Stone Soup tales

recipes for sharing

The Children's
Cabinet

Stone Soup tales
recipes for sharing
The Children's Cabinet

Published by Michalle Shown
for The Children's Cabinet, Inc.

Copyright © 2004 by
The Children's Cabinet, Inc.
1090 South Rock Blvd.
Reno, Nevada 89502
(775) 856-6200
www.childrenscabinet.org

This cookbook is a collection of favorite recipes and stories,
which are not necessarily original. Every attempt has been
made to acknowledge original authors where known.

ISBN: 0-9742785-0-5

Edited, designed, and manufactured by

CommunityClassics™
An imprint of

FRP

P.O. Box 305142
Nashville, Tennessee 37230
800 358-0560

Creative Design, Direction, and Editing by Michalle Shown
Original Cover Art by Jody Hunt, Design Factor
Logos and Creative Support by KPS/3

Manufactured in the United States of America

First Printing October 2003

2,500 copies

Contents

Acknowledgments

Our sincere thanks to the following individuals who helped grow this little seed of an idea into fabulous fruition.

Creative Design, Direction and Editing by Michalle Shown

Original Cover Art by Jody Hunt of Design Factor

Logos and Creative Support by KPS/3

Special thanks to Rose Sparks, whose assistance with organizing this project made it happen, Z Bahti for her administrative support, the Sandoval family and lots of our friends for sharing many family recipes, Mrs. Campbell's kindergarten class at Roy Gomm Elementary for their precious innocence and limitless imaginations, and to the management and staff of The Children's Cabinet, Inc., for their creative input and enthusiasm.

Dedication

This book is dedicated to our most precious natural resource, our children, and to our most endangered species, the family. Proceeds from this book will be dedicated to their service.

Many things we need can wait.

The child cannot.

Now is the time his bones are being formed;
His blood is being made;
his mind developed.

To him we cannot say tomorrow.

His name is today.

Gabriela Mistral

The Children's Cabinet, Inc.
a story of sharing

In 1985, local businessman Michael Dermody sought to create a high-level "Cabinet" of key public officials and prominent business leaders to address the needs of children in the community. A cross section of community leaders, representing local and state government, judiciary, child and family services, juvenile services, and social services, dedicated their time and expertise to this endeavor.

As a result of the commitment of these leaders, The Children's Cabinet, Inc., was established in December 1985 as a private nonprofit organization with the mission of creating a lasting public-private partnership to address the needs of children and families in our community. This unique commitment to public-private partnerships provides a foundation for The Cabinet's organizational strength by being able to respond quickly to the changing needs of the community and to bring about true collaboration in the delivery of service. Today, The Cabinet serves more than 15,000 children and families each year.

Over its history, The Cabinet has successfully brought diverse groups "to the table" to look at the issues facing children and families and develop innovative responses to meet those needs. In response to identified community needs, The Children's Cabinet has developed a number of programs over the years, including Parenting Education, Family Counseling, Reach for the Academic Difference Tutoring, and Truancy Prevention. The Cabinet has also started and spun off several successful programs, including the Adolescent Health Clinic, The Children's Cabinet in Incline Village, The Nevada Public Health Foundation, and Join Together. These programs are now either run by public agencies or are their own private, nonprofit organizations.

In 1995, The Children's Cabinet Staff and Trustees collaborated with other community organizations and obtained funding through state legislation which resulted in the creation of a network of nineteen Family Resource Centers (FRCs) throughout Nevada. The Cabinet provides technical assistance and oversight by serving as the Local Governing Board for all the Northern Nevada FRCs, which are currently located in Washoe, Lander, Storey, Elko, Lyon, Mineral, Churchill, Douglas, White Pine, and Humboldt Counties.

Since 1990, The Children's Cabinet has administered the State Welfare Division's Childcare Subsidy Program for all of Nevada except Clark, Esmeralda, and Nye Counties.

The Children's Cabinet, Inc., continues to meet the needs of children and families today with a vast and growing list of programs and services to include Child Care Subsidy Assistance, Early Literacy Programs, Family Counseling, the Caregiver Support Network, Employer Support Services, Quality Enhancement Programming, Respite Care, Community Education, the Runaway and Homeless Youth Mentoring and Equipping Program (RHYME), Teens Doing Stuff (TDS), RHYME to Prime (RTP), Project Walkabout, and the Computer Cabinet Technical Center.

Mission Statement

The Children's Cabinet is our community's stand to ensure every child and family has the services and resources to meet fundamental development, care and learning needs.

Stone Soup

a centuries-old Swedish fable of unknown origin

as retold by Michalle Shown

Sunshine warmed the forest and the last of the winter snow melted away. Forest animals started to peek out of their burrows, and tummies began to rumble. Rabbit was the first to stir.

The long lazy days of summer's end seemed so far gone now. He thought about how he had played until the last day of the season, long after his friends had stopped and begun preparing their winter stores.

His burrow was empty now and so was his tummy. "I'm so hungry. I'll have to find something. Perhaps I'll just beg from my friends. They'll be happy to share. They'll understand." But, soon he had asked everyone in the forest only to find that they weren't willing to share with the lazy Rabbit. They reminded him of how they had worked hard while he played and how they had planned ahead.

Dinnertime was drawing closer and closer, and Rabbit got a plan. "Well," he announced just loud enough for everyone to hear. "It's nearly dinnertime and I think I'll make a delicious pot of Stone Soup." The animals peeked out with curiosity and watched as Rabbit carefully selected a smooth round stone and set it into a pot full of water.

"Mmmm. Stone Soup. Why I haven't had Stone Soup since I was a wee bunny."

"Stone Soup?" inquired the Old Hare.

"My favorite!" replied Rabbit as he stirred and tasted. "I just wish I had a couple of carrots to add to the pot. Why surely you have an extra carrot hiding behind those long ears. That would make it perfect. Then we could share."

"I do have an extra carrot or two," replied Hare, and he scurried away to get them.

Bear and Badger had been watching from behind the tree. "Well, I have cubs to feed and they certainly would like a nice soup. All I have is meat," complained Bear.

"Why I suppose we could add meat to the Stone Soup and then there would be enough to share," offered Rabbit.

"And potatoes too," chimed in Badger eagerly.

Not to be left out, Skunk appeared with a large onion under his arm, followed closely by Porcupine carrying a cabbage. "We love Stone Soup!" they cried.

The animals took turns stirring and tasting until at last the soup was ready. They ate and laughed and ate some more. "This is wonderful. Who knew Stone Soup could be so delicious?" They all agreed.

"I believe it's the best I've ever made," smiled Rabbit.

Stone Soup

You will need:

1 medium stone about the size of a small fist (scrubbed clean and wrapped in foil)
1 cabbage (either red or green will do) cut into large pieces
2 medium onions cut-up
4 to 6 carrots cut into 1" pieces
4 potatoes cut-up
1 lb of tenderized stew beef cut-up
A handful of frozen peas
1 large can of tomato sauce
12 mushrooms cut in half (optional)
1 Tbsp of sage
1 Tbsp of parsley
Salt and pepper to taste

Brown the stew beef in a little oil and set aside. Fill a large soup pot a little over half full with water. Place it on the stovetop on medium heat. Add the stone. Add the tomato sauce. Season with sage, parsley, salt and pepper to taste. Bring seasoned stone to a boil and add cabbage, onions, carrots, potatoes, peas and mushrooms. Reduce heat to low, add stew meat and simmer 1 hour. Enjoy with piping hot French bread!

If You Make a Cookie FOR a Child

- it will show your love and care and it will surely be a treat

If You Make a Cookie WITH a Child

- you will help him/her feel helpful and important in the family
- you will help him/her feel that he/she can accomplish a task
- you will share a few precious moments together
- you will increase her/his feeling of self-worth
- you will help him/her learn about number concepts and measuring
- you will help him/her through a marvelous science experiment
- you will help him/her learn about sequencing (what goes 1st, 2nd, 3rd)
- you will improve her/his fine motor skills
- you will give him/her a chance to problem solve
- you will improve her/his understanding of words
- you will be helping him/her learn to read
- and it will show your love and care as well as surely being a treat

—Author unknown

Sharing the Kitchen . . .

Recipes you can prepare together

Green Eggs and Ham

4 eggs
2 ripe avocados, mashed
5 tablespoons water
2 slices precooked ham

Tools . . . . .2 skillets, measuring spoon, spoon,
tongs or fork, 2 plates

Ask . . . . .an adult to turn on the stove.

Scramble . . .the eggs, avocados and water quickly
in a skillet over high heat; do not let
the avocados brown.

Heat . . . . .the ham slices in a skillet.

Place . . . . . . .the ham on 2 plates.

Top . . . . .with the egg mixture.

Makes . . . . .2 servings

The **Children's
Cabinet**

12

Triple T Toast

2 teaspoons butter, softened
4 slices raisin bread or other bread
$1/4$ cup sugar
1 teaspoon cinnamon
$1/2$ cup applesauce, at room temperature
$1/2$ cup miniature marshmallows

Tools . . . . table knife, measuring spoon, measuring cup, bowl, wire rack, spoon, metal spatula, potholders

Spread . . . . . the butter on 1 side of the bread slices.

Mix . . . . the sugar and cinnamon in a small bowl. Sprinkle half the cinnamon mixture on the bread.

Ask . . . . an adult to turn on the toaster oven.

Toast . . . . . . the bread in a toaster oven. Transfer the toasted bread to a wire rack.

Spread . . . . . the applesauce on the bread and sprinkle with the remaining cinnamon mixture. Top with the marshmallows.

Return . . . . . to the toaster oven and toast until the marshmallows are golden brown.

Makes . . . . . 4 servings

Traditional Flour Tortillas by Nana

3 cups flour
$1/2$ teaspoon salt
$1/2$ teaspoon baking powder
$1/4$ cup vegetable oil
$3/4$ to 1 cup warm water

Tools . . . . .bowl, measuring cup, measuring spoon, plastic wrap or clean towel, griddle or cast-iron frying pan, rolling pin, metal spatula, sealable plastic bag or clean towel, food processor

Mix . . . . .the flour, salt and baking powder in a medium bowl with clean, dry hands.

Pour . . . . .in the oil and mix with hands until pea-size balls form.

Mix . . . . .in the warm water a little at a time until a soft dough forms.

Knead . . . . . .the dough on a lightly floured surface for 2 to 3 minutes or until it becomes smooth and elastic. Add a little more flour if the dough is sticky.

Place . . . . . . .the dough in a bowl and cover with plastic wrap or a clean towel. Let rest for 15 minutes.

Ask . . . . .an adult to heat a griddle or cast-iron frying pan over medium heat.

Form . . . . . .the dough into 1- to 2-inch balls.

Roll . . . . .out the balls as flat as possible with a rolling pin on a floured surface.

Cook . . . . . .the tortillas 1 at a time on the ungreased hot griddle.

Flip . . . . .the tortilla over when it starts to bubble, in about 15 to 20 seconds.

Cook . . . . . .on the other side.

Transfer . . . .the cooked tortillas to a sealable plastic bag or wrap in a towel to keep warm.

Serve . . . . . .with butter, cheese, eggs or your favorite cooked meat mixture.

Makes . . . . .12 to 16 tortillas

Note . . . . . . .This recipe is passed from generation to generation of children and grandchildren in the Rodriguez home. It is a tradition that shares proud cultural roots as well as some good cooking lessons. Making tortillas with Nana is a treat for the children and is almost always offered with a family story seasoned generously with Nana Carmen's wisdom.

by Carmen Rodriguez

Turtle Bread

Bread dough
2 raisins
1 egg
1 tablespoon water

Tools . . . . .ruler, baking sheet, knife, plastic wrap, small bowl, wire whisk, pastry brush, potholders, wire rack, metal spatula

Let . . . . .the dough rise once and punch down. Form into a 6-inch-diameter ball for the shell, a 3-inch-diameter ball for the head, 4 balls of 2 inches in diameter for legs and a strip of dough for the tail. Arrange on a greased baking sheet.

Make . . . . . . .a crisscross pattern on the shell with a knife. Place the raisins on the head for eyes. Cover with plastic wrap and let rise in a warm place for 30 minutes.

Ask . . . . .an adult to preheat the oven to 375 degrees.

Whisk . . . . . .the egg and water in a small bowl. Brush the egg mixture on the dough.

Bake . . . . . .for 25 minutes or until golden brown. Transfer to a wire rack using a spatula.

Makes . . . . .8 servings

Toad in the Hole

2 teaspoons butter, softened
1 slice bread
1 egg
Salt and pepper to taste

Tools . . . . . . .skillet, table knife, juice glass, metal spatula, plate

Ask . . . . .an adult to heat a skillet on the stove.

Spread . . . . .the butter on both sides of the bread.

Cut . . . . .a hole in the center of the bread with a small juice glass.

Place . . . . . .the bread and the cut-out hole piece in the skillet.

Break . . . . . .the egg into the hole.

Season . . . . .with salt and pepper.

Flip . . . . .the bread over when the egg turns white. Flip the hole piece, too.

Cook . . . . . .until the bread is golden brown on the other side.

Serve . . . . . .on a plate with the hole piece as a lid to cover the "toad."

Makes . . . . .1 serving

17

Freckle Faced Bears

1 (10-ounce) can refrigerated biscuits
$^{1}/_{4}$ cup sesame or sunflower seeds
12 raisins

Tools . . . . . . .measuring cup, waxed paper, baking
sheet, nonstick cooking spray,
potholders, wire rack, metal spatula

Ask . . . . .an adult to preheat the oven to
400 degrees.

Shape . . . . .6 dough biscuits into balls.

Sprinkle . . . .the sesame seeds onto waxed paper.

Roll . . . . .the dough balls in the sesame seeds,
coating well. Place far apart on a
baking sheet that has been coated
with nonstick cooking spray. Flatten
slightly to form bear heads.

Roll . . . . . . .small pieces of dough to make ears
and noses. Set the raisins on for eyes.

Use . . . . .any leftover dough to make fun
shapes such as letters or monsters.

Bake . . . . . .for 8 to 10 minutes or until golden brown.

Transfer . . . .the bears to a wire rack using a
metal spatula.

Makes . . . . .6 bears

Anthill Salad

2 apples, cored and cut into chunks
1 cup seedless grapes, cut into halves
1/2 cup raisins
1/2 cup miniature marshmallows
1 (8-ounce) container strawberry or
    strawberry-banana yogurt

Tools . . . . . . .medium bowl, measuring cup,
       wooden spoon

Combine . . .the apple chunks and grape halves in
       a medium bowl. Stir in the raisins and
       marshmallows with a wooden spoon.
       Add the yogurt, stirring to coat the fruit.

Makes . . . . .6 servings

Walkaround Salad

2 tablespoons peanut butter
1 teaspoon raisins
1 red or green apple, cored

Tools . . . . . . .measuring spoons, small bowl, spoon

Mix . . . . .the peanut butter and raisins in a small
       bowl. Stuff into the hollowed core of
       the apple.

Makes . . . . .1 serving

Heart-Tart Tea Sandwiches

1 sheet frozen puff pastry, thawed
6 small lettuce leaves
3/4 cup chicken salad or egg salad

Tools . . . . .heart-shaped cookie cutter, nonstick
baking sheet, potholders, metal spatula,
wire rack, fork, measuring cup, spoon

Ask . . . . .an adult to preheat the oven to 400
degrees.

Unfold . . . . . .the puff pastry on a lightly floured
surface. Cut out 6 hearts with a heart-
shaped cookie cutter.

Place . . . . . . .the hearts on a nonstick baking sheet.

Bake . . . . . . .for 12 to 15 minutes or until golden
brown.

Transfer . . . .the hearts to a wire rack using a metal
spatula and let cool completely.

Split . . . . .each cooled heart in half horizontally
into 2 layers with a fork.

Place . . . . . .a lettuce leaf on the bottom half of
each heart.

Spoon . . . . . . chicken salad on the lettuce and
cover with the top half of the heart.

Makes . . . . . .6 servings

Cookie Cutter Sandwiches

16 slices firm white bread
8 slices cooked turkey or ham
8 slices American cheese
Apples, cored and thinly sliced
Strawberries, sliced
Tub-style cream cheese (optional)

Tools . . . . . . .cutting board, cookie cutters, serving
platter, table knife

Place . . . . . . .the bread on a cutting board.

Cut . . . . .out desired shapes using cookie
cutters; set aside.

Set . . . . .the turkey and cheese on the
cutting board.

Cut . . . . .out the shapes using the same
cookie cutters.

Arrange . . . . .the bread, turkey, cheese, apples,
strawberries and cream cheese on
a serving platter.

Make . . . . . .into sandwiches, using a knife to
spread the cream cheese on
the bread.

Makes . . . . .8 servings

PB&J Backpacks

8 slices wheat or white bread
3/4 cup peanut butter
1/3 cup shredded apple
1/3 cup shredded carrot
1/8 teaspoon cinnamon

Tools . . . . . . .cutting board, serrated knife,
measuring spoon, measuring cup,
bowl, wooden spoon, table knife,
plastic wrap

Place . . . . . .the bread on a cutting board.

Cut . . . . .the crusts off the bread if desired.

Combine . . .the peanut butter, apple, carrot and
cinnamon in a bowl.

Stir. . . . . .with a wooden spoon to mix well.

Spread . . . . .on the bread slices.

Roll . . . . .the bread into backpack shapes.

Serve . . . . . .immediately or seal in plastic wrap
and chill for up to 24 hours.

Makes . . . . .8 servings

The **Children's Cabinet**

Peanut Butter Pizza

1 cup peanut butter
1 baked pizza crust
3 bananas, sliced
1/2 cup raisins

Tools . . . . .measuring cup, table knife, nonstick
baking sheet, potholders, metal
spatula, pizza cutter

Ask . . . . .an adult to preheat the oven to
350 degrees.

Spread . . . . .the peanut butter over the pizza crust.

Arrange . . . .the banana slices and raisins on top.

Place . . . . . .on a nonstick baking sheet.

Bake . . . . . .for 10 minutes or until the peanut
butter melts.

Transfer . . . .the pizza to a cutting board.

Slice . . . . . .and serve.

Makes . . . . .12 servings

Note . . . . . . .You may use a variety of fruits on the
pizza, such as strawberries, apples, or
blueberries.

The Children's
Cabinet

"I Am a Star" Pizza

1 (10-ounce) package refrigerated pizza
    dough
Shortening
1 (8-ounce) can pizza sauce
3 ounces pepperoni or Canadian bacon, sliced
5 slices mozzarella cheese
Grated Parmesan cheese

Tools . . . . .pizza cutter, baking sheet, measuring
spoon, wire rack, potholders, cookie
cutter, metal spatula

Ask . . . . .an adult to preheat the oven to
400 degrees.

Unroll . . . . . . .the pizza dough on a work surface. Cut
with a pizza cutter into 8 rectangles of
3x4-inches each.

Grease . . . . .a baking sheet with shortening.

Place . . . . . .the dough rectangles on the baking
sheet. Spread 2 teaspoons of pizza
sauce on each rectangle. Top with the
pepperoni.

Bake . . . . . .for 10 minutes. Transfer the baking
sheet to a wire rack.

Cut . . . . . . .the mozzarella cheese into star shapes
with a cookie cutter. Top each pizza
with a few cheese stars.

Sprinkle . . . .with Parmesan cheese. Bake for 2 to 3 minutes longer or until the cheese melts and the crust is golden brown.

Transfer . . . .the pizzas to a wire rack using a metal spatula and let cool for 5 minutes.

Makes . . . . .8 servings

English Muffin Pizzas

English muffins, split open
Pizza sauce
Favorite cooked meat topping
Favorite vegetable toppings
Shredded cheese

Tools . . . . . . .fork, spoon, nonstick baking sheet, potholders, wire rack, metal spatula

Ask . . . . .an adult to preheat the oven to 350 degrees.

Spread . . . . .pizza sauce on the split side of the English muffins. Top with meat and vegetables. Sprinkle with cheese.

Place . . . . . .on a nonstick baking sheet. Bake until the cheese melts.

Transfer . . . .to a wire rack using a metal spatula.

Mini-Pizzas

16 whole grain crackers
$1/4$ cup pizza sauce
$1/2$ cup shredded mozzarella cheese
Italian seasoning (optional)

Tools . . . . . . .measuring cup, nonstick baking sheet, table knife, potholders, metal spatula

Ask . . . . .an adult to preheat the oven to 350 degrees.

Arrange . . . .the crackers in a single layer on a nonstick baking sheet.

Spread . . . . .each cracker with $1/2$ to 1 teaspoon of the pizza sauce.

Sprinkle . . . .with cheese and Italian seasoning.

Bake . . . . . .for 5 minutes or until the cheese melts.

Makes . . . . .16 mini-pizzas

The **Children's Cabinet**

Three Blind Rice Mice

$1/4$ cup cooked rice
1 teaspoon cream cheese, softened
$1/2$ teaspoon plain yogurt
Pinch of salt
6 green peas
3 corn kernels
3 chives or thin strips of cheese
6 round pieces of olive, radish or cheese

Tools . . . . . . .measuring cup, measuring spoon, bowl, spoon, plate

Mix . . . . .the rice, cream cheese and yogurt in a small bowl.

Stir . . . . .in a pinch of salt.

Roll . . . . .the mixture into $1^1/2$-inch balls with slightly dampened hands and set on a plate.

Place . . . . . .the peas for eyes, the corn for the noses and the chives for tails.

Stick . . . . . . .in pieces of olive for ears.

Makes . . . . .3 mice

The **Children's Cabinet**

Funny Bagel Faces

1 carrot, sliced into rounds or shredded
Cherry tomatoes, halved
Sliced black olives
1 bell pepper, thinly sliced
1 cucumber, thinly sliced
Alfalfa sprouts
Grated beets (optional)
Minced chives (optional)
Toasted sunflower seeds (optional)
4 bagel halves
1 (8-ounce) tub-style cream cheese

Tools . . . . . . .small bowls, table knife

Arrange . . . .the vegetables and seeds in small bowls on a table.

Spread . . . . .the bagels with cream cheese.

Decorate . . .with the vegetables and seeds to make funny faces.

Makes . . . . .4 servings

The **Children's Cabinet**

Pretzel Candies

80 (approximately) round pretzel twists
1 (13-ounce) bag Hershey's Kisses, unwrapped
1 (5^1/$_4$-ounce) package "M&M's" Plain
   Chocolate Candies

Tools . . . . . . .baking sheet, foil, potholders

Ask . . . . .an adult to preheat the oven to
             275 degrees.

Arrange . . . .the pretzels in a single layer on a
             baking sheet lined with foil.

Place . . . . . . .1 kiss on top of each pretzel.

Bake . . . . . .for a few minutes or until the chocolate
             is soft but not melted.

Set . . . . .1 chocolate candy on top of each kiss
             and press gently a little into the soft
             chocolate.

Place . . . . . .in the freezer and freeze until hard.

Makes . . . . .80 candies

The Children's
Cabinet

Snowflake Sleds

6 (6-inch) flour tortillas
2 tablespoons butter, melted
2 tablespoons grated Parmesan cheese
$1/4$ teaspoon basil, crushed

Tools . . . . .cutting board, cookie cutters, pastry
brush, measuring spoon, small bowl,
spoon, nonstick baking sheet,
potholders, wire rack, metal spatula

Ask . . . . .an adult to preheat the oven to
375 degrees.

Place . . . . . . .the tortillas on a cutting board.

Make . . . . . . .cutouts in the tortillas with cookie
cutters to look like snowflakes. Brush
with the melted butter.

Mix . . . . .the cheese and basil in a small bowl.
Sprinkle over the snowflakes.

Arrange . . . . .the snowflakes on a nonstick baking
sheet. Bake for 10 to 12 minutes or until
golden brown.

Transfer . . . . .the snowflakes to a wire rack using a
metal spatula.

Makes . . . . . .6 servings

On-The-Trail Mix

2 cups chocolate-covered raisins
2 cups chopped dried fruit bits
1 cup dried cranberries
2 cups animal crackers
2 cups dry roasted peanuts

Tools . . . . .measuring cup, airtight container, wooden spoon

Combine . . .the raisins, dried fruit, animal crackers and peanuts in a large airtight container.

Stir . . . . .with a wooden spoon to mix well.

Seal . . . . .the container and store at room temperature for up to 3 months.

Makes . . . . . .16 ($1/2$-cup) servings

The **Children's Cabinet**

Fish in a Pond

4 ounces cream cheese, softened
Blue food coloring (optional)
Fish-shaped crackers
4 ribs celery

Tools . . . . . . .spoon, 2 bowls

Stir . . . . .the cream cheese in a bowl with the
food color to mix well.

Place . . . . . .the crackers in a bowl.

Dip . . . . .a celery rib in the cream cheese and
then into the crackers to "catch" a fish.

Makes . . . . .2 servings

The **Children's Cabinet**

Penguins

8 large dates, pitted
2 ounces cream cheese, softened
1 thin slice Cheddar cheese, cut into
    24 triangles
16 chocolate sprinkles

Tools . . . . .cutting board, knife, spoon, plate

Cut . . . . .the dates open lengthwise on a
                 cutting board.

Fill . . . . .the hollows with cream cheese.

Stand . . . . . .the dates up on a plate.

Place . . . . . . 2 Cheddar cheese triangles for feet
                 and 1 for a beak on each date to
                 make a penguin.

Put . . . . .2 sprinkles on each for eyes.

Makes . . . . .8 penguins

The Children's
Cabinet

Jello Shapes

1 package Jell-O, any flavor
Pieces of fruit
Whipped cream

Tools . . . . . . .measuring cup, spoon, heatproof bowl, large shallow pan, cookie cutters, plate

Ask . . . . .an adult to boil the amount of water on the gelatin package directions.

Stir . . . . .the boiling water into the gelatin in a heatproof bowl until dissolved.

Add . . . . . . .the amount of cold water on the gelatin package directions and stir to mix well.

Pour . . . . . . .into a large shallow pan or plastic container.

Chill . . . . . . .until firm.

Cut . . . . .out shapes with cookie cutters and place on a plate.

Decorate . . .the shapes with fruit and whipped cream.

The **Children's Cabinet**

34

Ladybugs on a Stick

Red seedless grapes, halved
Strawberries, hulled
Miniature chocolate chips
$1/2$ honeydew melon

Tools . . . . . . .wooden skewers

Push . . . . . . .half a grape on a short wooden skewer for the head.

Add . . . . . . .a strawberry body to the skewer.

Make . . . . . .marks on the strawberry with a fork to resemble wings.

Press . . . . . .miniature chocolate chips, tip end down, gently into the body for spots.

Repeat . . . . .to make as many ladybugs as desired.

Arrange . . . .the ladybugs on the melon.

The **Children's Cabinet**

Pretend Soup

2 cups orange juice
1/2 cup plain yogurt
1 tablespoon honey
2 teaspoons lemon juice
1 small banana, sliced
1 cup fresh or frozen berries
Additional favorite fruit, such as kiwifruit slices
    (optional)

Tools . . . . .measuring cup, measuring spoon,
        medium bowl, wire whisk, ladle,
        4 soup bowls

Combine . . .the orange juice, yogurt, honey and
        lemon juice in a medium bowl.

Whisk . . . . . .until it is all the same color.

Divide . . . . .the banana and berries among
        4 soup bowls.

Ladle . . . . . .the soup over the fruit.

Makes . . . . .4 servings

The **Children's Cabinet**

Pink Pig-Cicles

2 cups plain nonfat yogurt
1 (12-ounce) can frozen apple cranberry juice
    concentrate, thawed
2 teaspoons vanilla extract

Tools . . . . . . .measuring cup, measuring spoon, bowl,
    spoon, 8 paper cups, 8 plastic spoons

Combine . . .the yogurt, juice concentrate and
    vanilla in a bowl.

Stir . . . . .to mix well.

Pour . . . . . . .into small paper cups and insert plastic
    spoons for handles.

Freeze . . . . .until firm.

Run . . . . . . .hot water briefly over the outside of
    the cups to release the frozen pops.

Makes . . . . .8 pig-cicles

The **Children's Cabinet**

Cones of Surprise

1 (18$\frac{1}{4}$-ounce) package cake mix, batter
    made according to package directions,
    but not baked
24 flat-bottom ice cream cones
Frosting
Tinted sugar, sprinkles, cherries or candies
    for decoration

Tools . . . . . . .measuring cup, spoon, baking pan,
              potholders, wire rack, table knife

Ask . . . . .an adult to preheat the oven.

Spoon . . . . .the cake batter into the ice cream
              cones, filling $2/3$ full.

Set . . . . .the cones in a baking pan.

Bake . . . . . .according to package directions
              for cupcakes.

Remove . . . .the cones to a wire rack.

Frost . . . . . . .the cones when cool.

Decorate . . .with sugar, sprinkles, cherries or candies.

Makes . . . . .24 cones

The **Children's Cabinet**

38

No-Bake Cookies

$1/4$ cup ($1/2$ stick) butter
$3/4$ cup granulated sugar
$1/4$ cup packed brown sugar
$1/4$ cup milk
$1/4$ cup baking cocoa
$1/8$ teaspoon salt
$1/4$ cup peanut butter
$1/8$ teaspoon vanilla extract
$1 1/2$ cups quick-cooking oats
$1/4$ cup flour

Tools . . . . . . .measuring cup, measuring spoon, saucepan, spoon, waxed paper

Ask . . . . .an adult to turn on the stove.

Combine . . .the butter, granulated sugar, brown sugar, milk, baking cocoa and salt in a saucepan. Bring to a boil.

Boil . . . . .for 1 minute and remove from the heat.

Add . . . . . . .the peanut butter, vanilla, oats and flour. Stir to mix well.

Drop . . . . . . .by spoonfuls onto waxed paper. Chill until firm.

Makes . . . . .3 dozen cookies

Cookie Puppets

2 3/4 cups flour
3/4 teaspoon baking soda
1/2 teaspoon salt
1 cup (2 sticks) butter, softened
1 cup sugar
1 egg
1 tablespoon vanilla extract
Frosting
Assorted candies

Tools . . . . .measuring cup, measuring spoon, medium bowl, large bowl, electric mixer, plastic wrap, rolling pin, wide-mouth glass, cookie sheets, 15 to 18 lollipop sticks, potholders, wire rack, metal spatula, pastry bag

Stir . . . . .the flour, baking soda and salt in a medium bowl.

Beat . . . . . . .the butter and sugar in a large bowl with an electric mixer for 1 minute.

Add . . . . .the egg and vanilla and beat well.

Beat . . . . .in the dry ingredients gradually until well mixed. The dough will be stiff.

Divide . . . . . .the dough into 2 balls and flatten each into a disk. Cover with plastic wrap. Chill for at least 2 hours or overnight.

Place . . . . . . .1 disk of dough on plastic wrap and cover with a piece of plastic wrap. Roll with a rolling pin to $^1/_4$-inch thickness. Remove the top layer of plastic wrap.

Cut . . . .$3^1/_2$-inch-diameter circles with a wide-mouth glass.

Place . . . . . .on ungreased cookie sheets.

Insert . . . . . .a lollipop stick in the center of each cookie. Repeat with remaining disk of dough. Chill for 30 minutes.

Ask . . . . .an adult to preheat the oven to 350 degrees.

Bake . . . . . .the cookies for 8 to 10 minutes or until golden brown around the edges. Let cool on the cookie sheets for 5 minutes.

Transfer . . . .the cookies to a wire rack using a metal spatula and let cool.

Spoon . . . . .frosting into a pastry bag.

Pipe . . . . . . .frosting on the cookies to make eyes, mouth and hair or decorate with candy using frosting to anchor the candy features.

Makes . . . . .15 to 18 puppets

Dirt Cake

1 (32-ounce) package chocolate sandwich
   cookies
8 ounces cream cheese, softened
1 cup confectioners' sugar
2 ($3^1/2$-ounce) packages instant vanilla or
   chocolate pudding mix
$3^1/2$ cups milk
12 ounces whipped topping
Candy worms

Tools . . . . .sealable plastic bag, rolling pin,
measuring cup, spoon, large bowl,
medium bowl, new 8-inch flowerpot
or 8 to 10 new small flowerpots,
plastic flowers

Place . . . . the cookies in a sealable plastic bag
and seal tightly.

Crush . . . . . .with a rolling pin into small pieces.

Stir . . . . .the cream cheese and confectioners'
sugar in a large bowl until smooth.

Mix . . . . .the pudding mix, milk and whipped
topping in a medium bowl.

The **Children's
Cabinet**

Add . . . . .to the cream cheese mixture and stir
to blend.

Set . . . . .aside 1 to 2 cups of cookie crumbs.

Add . . . . . . .the remaining crumbs and a few
candy worms to the cream cheese
mixture.

Stir . . . . .to mix well.

Pour . . . . . . .into an 8-inch-diameter x 10-inch-deep
flowerpot or 8 to 10 small flowerpots.

Sprinkle . . . .with the reserved crushed cookies.

Chill . . . . . . .for 2 hours.

Decorate . . .with additional candy worms and
plastic flowers.

Makes . . . . .8 to 10 servings

Note . . . . . . .Boil the flowerpot in a large saucepan
of water to sterilize and let cool before
filling with the cake.

The **Children's**
Cabinet

Campfire Fruit Kabobs

2 bananas, cut into 16 pieces
16 pineapple chunks
2 nectarines, cut into 16 pieces
8 red maraschino cherries
1/2 cup strawberry jam
1/2 cup chocolate syrup

Tools . . . . . . .8 metal skewers, measuring cup, bowl, spoon, pastry brush, potholders, plate

Ask . . . . .an adult to prepare a grill or campfire for direct grilling.

Thread . . . . .2 pieces of banana, 2 pineapple chunks and 2 pieces of nectarine on each of 8 metal skewers.

Place . . . . . . .1 cherry on the end of each skewer.

Stir . . . . .the jam in a small bowl until softened. Brush jam on each kabob.

Place . . . . . .the kabobs on the grill rack over medium-hot coals or on a rack 3 to 4 inches above the campfire.

Grill . . . . . . .for 2 minutes. Turn the kabobs over using potholders. Grill for 2 minutes longer.

Transfer . . . .the kabobs to a plate using potholders. Drizzle with chocolate syrup.

Makes . . . . .8 servings

Backyard Banana Boats

4 unpeeled bananas

1 (1^1/2-ounce) milk chocolate bar, broken
    into pieces

^{1}/2 cup miniature marshmallows

4 scoops vanilla ice cream

Tools . . . . . . .knife, measuring cup, foil, long-handled
tongs, potholders

Ask . . . . .an adult to prepare a grill or campfire
for direct grilling.

Slice . . . . . . .through the inside curve of each
banana almost to the inside edge
of the peel on the other side.

Insert . . . . . .the chocolate pieces and miniature
marshmallows into the slits.

Close . . . . . .the bananas and wrap tightly in foil
with the closing at the top of the slit.

Grill . . . . . . .for 4 to 5 minutes over a medium-hot fire.

Transfer . . . .from the grill to plates with long-
handled tongs.

Open . . . . . .the foil, add a scoop of ice cream to
each hot banana and enjoy.

Makes . . . . .4 servings

by Michalle Shown

Apple Spice I-Did-It-Myself Cake

1 (18¹/₄-ounce) package spice cake mix
2 (21-ounce) cans apple pie filling
Confectioners' sugar
Vanilla ice cream (optional)

Tools . . . . . . .bowl, spoon, nonstick cooking spray, bundt pan, potholders, wire rack, serving plate

Ask . . . . .an adult to preheat the oven to 350 degrees.

Combine . . .the cake mix and pie filling in a bowl.

Stir . . . . .to mix well.

Spoon . . . . .into a bundt pan generously coated with nonstick cooking spray.

Bake . . . . . .for 45 to 50 minutes.

Transfer . . . .to a wire rack and let cool in the pan for 10 minutes.

Invert . . . . . .onto a serving plate and let cool.

Dust . . . . . . .with confectioners' sugar.

Serve . . . . . .with vanilla ice cream.

Makes . . . . .6 to 8 servings

The Children's
Cabinet

Apple Fondue

1/2 cup chunky peanut butter
1/4 cup crisp rice cereal
2 tablespoons raisins
2 green apples, cut into wedges

Tools . . . . . . .measuring cup, measuring spoon, small
bowl, spoon

Mix . . . . .the peanut butter, cereal and raisins in
a small bowl. Dip the apple wedges in
the thick peanut butter mixture.

Makes . . . . .2 servings

Chilly Willy Sandwich

1/4 cup favorite yogurt
1 waffle
1/4 cup favorite fresh fruit

Tools . . . . . . .measuring cup, table knife, plastic wrap

Spread . . . . .the yogurt on the waffle. Top with the
fruit.

Fold . . . . . . .in half and wrap tightly in plastic wrap.

Freeze . . . . .until firm.

Makes . . . . .1 serving

PB and Banana Pudding

3 bananas, sliced
$1/2$ cup applesauce
2 teaspoons peanut butter
$1/4$ cup orange juice

Tools . . . . . . .measuring cup, measuring spoon, blender, 4 small bowls

Combine . . .the bananas, applesauce, peanut butter and orange juice in a blender container.

Process . . . .until smooth.

Serve . . . . . .in small bowls or cups.

Makes . . . . .4 ($1/2$-cup) servings

The **Children's Cabinet**

Peanut Butter Cups

2 cups confectioners' sugar
1 cup peanut butter
$1/2$ cup (1 stick) butter, melted
1 package almond bark

Tools . . . . .measuring cup, 2 spoons, bowl, double
boiler, paper cupcake liners, airtight
container

Combine . . . .the confectioners' sugar, peanut butter
and melted butter in a bowl. Stir to mix
well. Chill for 1 hour. Roll into small balls.

Ask . . . . .an adult to turn on the stove.

Melt . . . . .the almond bark in the top of a
double boiler over simmering water.

Arrange . . . .paper cupcake liners on a baking
sheet.

Spoon . . . . . .a small amount of melted almond bark
to cover the bottom of each cup.

Place . . . . . . .a peanut butter ball on top.

Cover . . . . . .with more melted chocolate so that
no peanut butter is showing. Freeze
until firm.

Store . . . . . .in an airtight container in the freezer.

Makes . . . . .15 to 18 cups

Crispy Rice Cereal Treats

2 tablespoons butter
2 cups miniature marshmallows
3 cups crispy rice cereal

Tools . . . . .measuring cup, large saucepan, spoon, wooden spoon, 9x13-inch pan, nonstick cooking spray, spatula, table knife

Melt . . . . .the butter in a large saucepan over low heat.

Add . . . . .the marshmallows.

Cook . . . . . . .until completely melted, stirring constantly.

Remove . . . . .from the heat and add the cereal.

Stir . . . . .with a wooden spoon until the cereal is well coated.

Spoon . . . . . .the mixture into a 9x13-inch pan coated with nonstick cooking spray.

Press . . . . . . .evenly over the bottom of the pan with a spatula coated with nonstick cooking spray.

Cut . . . . .into 2-inch squares when cool.

Makes . . . . .24 to 30 squares

Ducky Dessert

Favorite flavor ice cream
2 chocolate chips or raisins
1 orange gumdrop, flattened and cut into
    2 pieces
Fruit leather or dried apricots

Tools . . . . . . .small plate or bowl, paper cupcake
                liner, ice cream scoop, spoon, knife

Spread . . . . .a paper cupcake liner on a small plate
                or in a bowl.

Place . . . . . .large scoop of ice cream for the body
                on the liner.

Flatten . . . . .the top slightly with the back of
                a spoon.

Set . . . . .a small scoop of ice cream on top for
                the head.

Press . . . . . .in chocolate chips or raisins for eyes
                and the gumdrop pieces for a beak.

Add . . . . . . .webbed feet with fruit leather or dried
                apricots.

Makes . . . . .1 serving

The Children's
Cabinet

Marshmallow Snowmen

Wedges of baked angel food cake
Whipped cream
Thin pretzel sticks
Large marshmallows
Candy pieces
Fruit leather
Gumdrops
Black licorice sticks

Tools . . . . . . .plate, spoon, knife

Place . . . . . . .a wedge of angel food cake on a plate. Cover with whipped cream "snow."

Push . . . . . . .pretzel stick through 3 marshmallows to create a snowman body.

Attach . . . . . .2 pretzels in the sides for arms.

Press . . . . . . .pieces of candy on the snowman for eyes, nose, mouth and buttons.

Tie . . . . .on a fruit leather "scarf."

Set . . . . .a gumdrop on top for a hat.

Place . . . . . .licorice "skis" on the snow.

Anchor . . . .the snowman on top of the skis with a pretzel stick.

Repeat . . . . .to make as many snowmen as desired.

Smoothie Pops

5 strawberries, hulled
1 banana
1 cup strawberry yogurt
$1/2$ cup milk
$1/2$ cup fruit juice
4 ice cubes

Tools . . . . . . .measuring cup, blender, 3-ounce paper cups, plastic wrap, popsicle sticks

Combine . . .the strawberries, banana, yogurt, milk, juice and ice cubes in a blender container.

Process . . . .until smooth.

Pour . . . . . . .into 3-ounce paper cups and cover with plastic wrap.

Insert . . . . . .a popsicle stick in the center of each cup.

Freeze . . . . .for at least 5 hours.

Makes . . . . .12 pops

The **Children's Cabinet**

Green Monster-Ade

1^1/2 cups apple juice
1 (3-ounce) package lime gelatin
1^1/2 cups apple juice
3 cups orange drink, chilled

Tools . . . . .measuring cup, saucepan, wooden
spoon, pitcher, 6 glasses

Ask . . . . .an adult to turn on the stove.

Stir . . . . .the 1^1/2 cups apple juice and gelatin
with a wooden spoon in a saucepan.

Cook . . . . . . .over low heat until the gelatin
dissolves, stirring constantly.

Remove . . . . .from the heat and stir in 1^1/2 cups
apple juice.

Pour . . . . .into a pitcher.

Chill . . . . .for 1^1/2 to 2 hours or until slightly
thickened.

Divide . . . . . .the mixture evenly among 6 glasses.

Pour . . . . . . .1/2 cup of orange drink slowly down
the side of each glass so that it floats
on top of the green layer.

Makes . . . . .6 servings

Orange Julius Frappe

$^1/_3$ cup frozen orange juice concentrate
$^1/_2$ cup milk
$^1/_2$ cup water
$^1/_4$ cup sugar
$^1/_2$ teaspoon vanilla extract
5 or 6 ice cubes

Tools . . . . . . .measuring cup, measuring spoon, blender

Combine . . .the orange juice concentrate, milk, water, sugar, vanilla and ice cubes in a blender container.

Process . . . .for 30 seconds or until smooth.

Makes . . . . .1 or 2 servings

by Rose Sparks

The Children's Cabinet

The Crow and the Pitcher of Water

A fable from northern India, retold by Rohini Chowdhury

In the spreading branches of a leafy, old neem tree there lived a wise old crow. All day long he would fly over towns and villages in search of food. He would meet other birds and animals, make friends, and gather news. In the evenings he would return to his home in the old tree, content with the way his day had been spent.

One year, the rains were late, and the land was hit by a terrible drought. The water in the ponds and lakes and rivers began to dry up. Birds, animals, and even people were dying of thirst. The pond on the banks of which the neem tree grew was shrinking every day, until one morning it vanished completely. The crow was worried—how long could he carry on?

He flew all day in search of water. He had almost given up, when he suddenly saw an old earthen pitcher lying half-buried in the dried-up mud of a village pond. At the very bottom of the pitcher there was water. But the pitcher was deep, its neck too narrow, and the crow could not reach the water. What was he to do?

The crow looked around and saw that the ground was strewn with pebbles. He began to throw pebble after pebble into the pitcher until the water in it had risen enough for him to drink.

The resourceful crow had enough water for a week— and the rains came after all. He did not give up even when it seemed impossible. If you try hard enough, even the most difficult problems can be solved. The important thing is to not give up trying.

Recipes Your Whole Family Will Love . . .

Favorite family recipes for Soups, Salads
and Sides; Entrées and Main Dishes;
Desserts and Beverages

Zigzag Walk

As retold by Heather Forest

Under the waves at the bottom of the sea, a mother crab scolded her daughter.

"Why are you scurrying side to side in that ridiculous zigzag walk of yours? Come forward! Walk straight, like other creatures do!"

"But mother," squeaked the little crab, "I learned to walk from you! If you want something different of me…change the example I see!"

And with that, the little crab zig-zig-zigzagged away.

Soups, Salads and Sides

Easy Cheesy Quesadilla

2 tablespoons refried beans
2 flour tortillas
$1/2$ cup shredded Monterey Jack cheese

Spread the beans on 1 tortilla. Sprinkle with the cheese. Heat a skillet over medium-high heat. Place the tortilla in the skillet and top with the remaining tortilla. Cook for 45 seconds. Flip the quesadilla and cook for 45 seconds on the other side or until golden brown. Remove to a plate and let cool slightly.
Yield: 1 serving.

Cowboy Caviar

1 (15-ounce) can black beans, rinsed and drained
1 (4-ounce) can black olives, drained
1 small onion, finely chopped (about $1/4$ cup)
1 garlic clove, minced
2 tablespoons vegetable oil
3 tablespoons lime juice
$1/4$ teaspoon salt
$1/4$ teaspoon crushed red pepper
$1/4$ teaspoon cumin
$1/8$ teaspoon black pepper
8 ounces cream cheese, softened
2 hard-cooked eggs, chopped
1 green onion, chopped

Combine the beans, olives, onion, garlic, oil, lime juice, salt, red pepper, cumin and black pepper in a bowl. Stir to mix well. Cover and chill for at least 2 hours. Spread the cream cheese on a serving plate. Spoon the bean mixture evenly over the cream cheese. Arrange the chopped eggs in a ring on top of the bean mixture and sprinkle with the green onion. *Yield: 12 servings.*

by Patricia Lynn

The **Children's Cabinet**

Ham and Asparagus Wraps

8 ounces cream cheese, softened
8 thin slices cooked ham
8 pickled asparagus spears

Spread the cream cheese on the ham slices. Place 1 asparagus spear on the edge of each slice and roll up. *Yield: 8 servings.*

Ham Roll-Ups

3 ounces cream cheese, softened
1/2 cup shredded Cheddar cheese
1 tablespoon chopped green onions
1 teaspoon prepared mustard
8 slices cooked ham

Mix the cream cheese, Cheddar cheese, green onions and mustard in a bowl until blended. Spread on the ham slices and roll up. Cut into pieces and insert a wooden pick in each piece. Arrange on a microwave-safe plate. Microwave on High for 10 to 20 seconds. *Yield: 32 pieces.*

by Rose Sparks

Torrejas (Torta de Huevo)

4 egg yolks
3 tablespoons flour
1/2 teaspoon baking powder
Pinch of salt
4 egg whites
Vegetable oil for deep-frying
Red chili sauce

Beat the egg yolks, flour, baking powder and salt in a bowl until well mixed. Beat the egg whites in a large bowl until stiff peaks form. Fold in the egg yolk mixture. Drop by spoonfuls into hot oil in a skillet. Fry until golden brown on both sides. Remove to paper towels to drain. Serve covered with red chili sauce. *Yield: 4 servings.*

Easy Cheesy Chili Dip

1 pound ground beef
1 onion, finely chopped
2 tablespoons masa flour
2 tablespoons chili powder
1/2 teaspoon cumin
1/4 teaspoon oregano
1/2 cup strong beef broth
Cayenne pepper to taste
12 ounces Velveeta cheese, cubed

Brown the ground beef with the onion in a skillet, stirring until the ground beef is crumbly; drain. Stir in the next 5 ingredients. Season with cayenne pepper. Simmer for 30 minutes or until thickened. Add the cheese and simmer until the cheese melts, stirring frequently. Remove from the heat and let cool slightly. Chill, covered, overnight. Reheat and serve with tortilla chips. *Yield: 4 cups.*

Bright Pink Fruit Dip

1 (10-ounce) package frozen raspberries with syrup, thawed
4 ounces cream cheese, softened
1 cup firm yogurt
2 teaspoons lemon juice
Spears of cantaloupe or honeydew melon
Spears of firm banana
Slices of apple or pear

Purée the raspberries with syrup in a blender or food processor. Add the cream cheese and process until blended. Remove to a bowl and whisk in the yogurt and lemon juice until well mixed. Pour into a serving bowl and place in the center of a serving plate. Arrange the fruit on the plate around the dip. Dunk the fruit into the dip and pop it in your mouth! *Yield: 4 or 5 snack servings.*

Note: If using fresh or frozen unsweetened raspberries, add 2 to 3 tablespoons of sugar or honey or to taste.

Clam Dip

1 (6$^{1}/_{2}$-ounce) can minced clams
6 ounces cream cheese, softened
1 (12-ounce) carton cottage cheese
2 tablespoons mayonnaise
Garlic salt to taste

Drain the clams, reserving the liquid. Beat the cream cheese in a bowl with an electric mixer until light and fluffy. Beat in the cottage cheese, mayonnaise and clams. Season with garlic salt. Beat in the reserved clam liquid gradually. Cover and chill. *Yield: 3 cups.*

by Rose Sparks

Tomato Salsa

3 tomatoes
1 small green bell pepper
1 jalapeño chile
6 green onions, finely chopped
3 garlic cloves, minced
2 tablespoons chopped fresh cilantro
2 tablespoons fresh lime juice
$^{1}/_{2}$ teaspoon salt
Flour tortillas or tortilla chips

Cut the tomatoes into halves on a cutting board. Squeeze each half cut side down to remove the seeds. Chop the tomatoes and place in a bowl. Cut the bell pepper into halves lengthwise and remove the stem, seeds and membrane. Chop the bell pepper and add to the tomatoes. Cut the jalapeño into halves lengthwise and remove the stem, seeds and membrane. Chop the jalapeño finely and add to the tomatoes. Stir in the green onions, garlic, cilantro, lime juice and salt. Cover and chill for at least 1 hour or for up to 7 days. Serve with tortillas or tortilla chips or as an accompaniment to chicken, fish or other main dishes. *Yield: 3$^{1}/_{2}$ cups.*

Note: To avoid irritating burning oils, wash your hands and utensils well in soapy water after handling jalapeño chiles. Do not touch your face or eyes until the oils have been washed from your hands.

Heart-y Veggie Dip

4 ounces cream cheese, softened
1 cup favorite sour cream dip
1 tablespoon (about) milk
1 unsliced round loaf sourdough bread
1/2 cup prepared salsa
Bite-size fresh vegetables for dipping

Beat the cream cheese with a wooden spoon in a bowl until smooth. Stir in half the dip. Add the remaining dip and enough milk to make of a dipping consistency and stir to mix well. Place the bread on a work surface. Mark a large heart shape on top of the bread with a serrated knife. Cut out the heart, cutting almost to but not through the bottom of the bread. Lift out the bread heart carefully and save for another use. Hollow out the bread with a spoon, leaving a 1/2-inch shell of bread. Spoon the dip into the shell. Top with the salsa. Serve with the fresh vegetables.
Yield: 6 servings.

ABC Vegetable Soup

1/2 cup chopped onion
1 garlic clove, minced
1 teaspoon vegetable oil
2 (14-ounce) cans chicken broth
1 (28-ounce) can crushed tomatoes
1/3 cup alphabet pasta
1/2 cup chopped fresh parsley
1 cup each chopped broccoli and carrots
1 cup sliced celery
Salt and pepper to taste
Grated Parmesan cheese

Sauté the onion and garlic in hot oil in a large saucepan over medium heat for 2 minutes or until the onion is tender. Stir in the broth, tomatoes, pasta and parsley. Bring to a boil. Simmer for 10 minutes. Add the broccoli, carrots and celery. Cook for 10 minutes. Season with salt and pepper. Ladle the soup into serving bowls and sprinkle with cheese. *Yield: 6 servings.*

Minestrone

4 ounces lean salt pork, diced
4 cups beef broth
1 cup cubed peeled potatoes
1 cup coarsely chopped carrots
1 cup cubed turnips
3/4 cup uncooked rice
1 cup sliced onion
1/2 cup lima beans
1/2 cup green peas
1/4 head cabbage, shredded
4 ounces fresh spinach, shredded
1 leek (white part only), halved lengthwise, sliced crosswise
1/2 cup coarsely chopped celery
4 tomatoes, chopped
2 tablespoons tomato paste
2 tablespoons chopped fresh parsley
1/2 teaspoon ground sage
1/2 teaspoon pepper
Salt to taste
Grated Parmesan cheese

Place the salt pork in a large saucepan and add just enough water to cover. Simmer, covered, for 30 minutes. Add the beef broth and return to a boil. Stir in the potatoes, carrots, turnips and rice. Cover and cook for 10 minutes. Add the onion, lima beans, peas, cabbage, spinach, leek, celery, tomatoes, tomato paste, parsley, sage and pepper. Season with salt. Bring to a boil slowly. Cook, uncovered, for 1 hour or until the soup is very thick and the vegetables are tender. Ladle into serving bowls and sprinkle with cheese. *Yield: 12 main-dish servings.*

The **Children's Cabinet**

Cheesy Corn Chowder

1 (15$\frac{1}{4}$-ounce) can whole kernel corn
2 potatoes, peeled and cubed
1 cup chopped celery
3 cups chicken broth
$\frac{1}{2}$ teaspoon Tabasco sauce
Salt to taste
2 tablespoons butter
3 tablespoons flour
2 cups milk
1$\frac{1}{4}$ cups shredded Cheddar cheese
1 red bell pepper, chopped

Combine the corn, potatoes, celery, broth and Tabasco sauce in a large saucepan. Season with salt. Bring to a boil and reduce the heat. Simmer, covered, for 30 minutes or until the potatoes are tender. Melt the butter in a heavy saucepan. Stir in the flour. Cook for 1 minute, stirring constantly; do not let brown. Stir in the milk gradually. Cook until the mixture thickens and comes to a boil, stirring constantly. Add to the corn mixture. Stir in the cheese and bell pepper. Cook over low heat until the cheese is melted, stirring frequently. *Yield: 4 servings.*

Snowball Soup

2 carrots, sliced
2 ribs celery, chopped
5 cups chicken broth
$\frac{1}{8}$ teaspoon pepper
1$\frac{1}{2}$ cups chopped cooked chicken
1$\frac{1}{2}$ cups baking mix
$\frac{1}{2}$ cup milk

Combine the carrots, celery, broth and pepper in a large saucepan. Bring to a boil over high heat. Simmer, covered, over medium-low heat for 10 minutes. Stir in the chicken. Combine the baking mix and milk in a bowl. Stir to mix well. Spoon the dough in 12 mounds on top of the soup. Cook, covered, for 10 minutes or until a wooden pick inserted in a dumpling comes out clean. *Yield: 6 servings.*

One Potato, Two Potato

3 potatoes, peeled and chopped
5 cups water
2 tablespoons butter
1 small leek (white and pale green part only), chopped
1 green bell pepper, chopped
1 tablespoon chopped fresh parsley
$1/2$ teaspoon salt
$1/2$ teaspoon pepper
6 slices bacon, crisp-cooked and crumbled
Bread crumbs or croutons

Combine the potatoes and water in a saucepan. Bring to a boil and cook for 15 minutes or until the potatoes are tender. Drain and reserve the cooking liquid. Melt the butter in a large saucepan over medium heat. Add the leek, bell pepper, parsley, salt and pepper. Sauté for 5 minutes. Stir in half the potatoes and half the cooking liquid. Bring to a boil and reduce the heat. Simmer for 15 minutes. Remove from the heat and let cool slightly. Purée 1 cup of the soup in a blender. Add up to $1/2$ cup of cooking liquid if the soup is too thick to purée. Return the puréed soup to the saucepan. Stir in the remaining potatoes and cooking liquid. Cook until heated through. Ladle into serving bowls. Mix the crumbled bacon and bread crumbs in a bowl. Sprinkle on top of the soup. *Yield: 4 to 6 servings.*

Note: You may use 2 tablespoons of bacon drippings instead of butter to sauté the vegetables.

The **Children's Cabinet**

Matzo Ball Soup

1 chicken, whole or cut up
2 onions, cut into pieces
2 carrots, cut into pieces
3 ribs celery, cut into pieces
2 tablespoons butter, melted
2 eggs, lightly beaten
1/2 cup matzo meal
2 tablespoons soup or water
1/2 teaspoon salt
Dried parsley flakes to taste
Onion powder and/or garlic powder to taste
1 tablespoon salt, or to taste

Simmer the chicken, onions, carrots and celery with enough water to cover in a large saucepan for 3 hours or until the chicken is tender, skimming the foam as needed. Pour the soup through a colander into a large saucepan. Remove the chicken from the bones and add to the soup or reserve for another use. Purée the cooked vegetables in a blender with a small amount of water. Add to the soup. Cover and chill overnight.

Mix the next 7 ingredients in a bowl. Cover and chill for 15 minutes. Form into small balls. Skim the fat from the surface of the soup. Stir in 1 tablespoon salt. Bring to a boil. Drop the matzo balls into the soup. Reduce the heat and cover. Simmer for 30 minutes or until the matzo balls rise to the surface. *Yield: 12 servings.*

Carrot and Raisin Sunshine Salad

5 to 6 carrots, shredded
1/2 cup raisins
8 ounces low-fat vanilla yogurt
4 to 6 iceberg lettuce leaves

Stir the carrots, raisins and yogurt in a bowl. Cover and chill for 15 minutes. Toss to mix. Place a lettuce leaf on each serving plate and top with the carrot salad. *Yield: 4 to 6 servings.*

Carrot Pennies

2 thin carrots, sliced into rounds
1 teaspoon butter
3 shakes of salt
1 squeeze lemon juice
1 tablespoon brown sugar
1 teaspoon sesame seeds
$^1/_4$ cup water

Steam the carrots or boil in a small amount of water in a saucepan until barely tender; drain. Return to the saucepan. Add the butter, salt, lemon juice, brown sugar, sesame seeds and water. Cook over medium heat until the carrots are coated, stirring constantly. Add more sugar or water if desired. *Yield: 3 to 4 snack servings.*

Pineapple Candle Salad

Lettuce leaves
Canned pineapple rings
Bananas, cut into halves
Carrot
Nuts and pieces of other fruit, if desired

Arrange a lettuce leaf on each serving plate and top with a pineapple ring. Cut the pointed end off the bananas and stand half a banana in the center of each ring. Peel strips of carrot and form each strip into a circle, overlapping the ends. Place 1 end of a wooden pick through the overlapped edges and the other end into the top of the banana. Pinch the carrot circle flame to make it more pointed. Decorate the candle with nuts and pieces of fruit.

The Children's Cabinet

Crispy Winter Vegetable Salad

1 (16-ounce) bag salad mix
4 cups broccoli florets
2 carrots, thinly sliced
3 red bell peppers, thinly sliced
1 bunch radishes, halved
2 ribs celery, thinly sliced
3 (8-ounce) bottles Italian salad dressing

Combine the salad mix, broccoli, carrots, bell peppers, radishes and celery in a large bowl. Toss to mix. Add the salad dressing and toss to coat. *Yield: 10 servings.*

Calabasitas (Sautéed Zucchini)

1 onion, chopped
1 garlic clove, minced
2 zucchini, chopped
$1/4$ teaspoon salt
$1/8$ teaspoon pepper
Pinch of dried rosemary, crushed

Sauté the onion and garlic in a nonstick skillet until tender. Add the zucchini, salt, pepper and rosemary, Sauté for 6 to 8 minutes or until the zucchini is tender-crisp. *Yield: 3 or 4 servings.*

The **Children's Cabinet**

Gold Coin Potatoes

3 potatoes, peeled and sliced into $1/4$- to $1/2$-inch rounds
2 tablespoons olive oil or vegetable oil
$1/8$ teaspoon basil, crushed
$1/8$ teaspoon pepper
$1/4$ to $1/2$ cup shredded American or Cheddar cheese

Preheat the oven to 450 degrees. Place the potatoes in a sealable plastic bag. Drizzle with the olive oil and sprinkle with the basil and pepper. Seal the bag and shake to coat the potatoes. Arrange the potatoes in a single layer on a nonstick baking sheet. Bake at 450 degrees for 25 minutes or until golden brown. Remove the potatoes to a serving platter. Sprinkle the cheese over the potatoes. Let stand for 2 to 3 minutes for the cheese to melt. *Yield: 6 servings.*

Baked Spanish Rice

1 cup uncooked rice
1 teaspoon salt
1 large onion, chopped
1 large green bell pepper, chopped
1 tablespoon butter
2 cups chopped canned tomatoes
$1/2$ teaspoon pepper
Shredded Cheddar or Colby cheese

Cook the rice with the salt according to package directions. Combine the onion, bell pepper and butter in a microwave-safe baking dish. Microwave on High for 3 minutes, stirring once. Add the cooked rice, tomatoes and pepper to the baking dish. Stir to mix well. Sprinkle with Cheddar cheese to liberally cover the rice mixture. Bake at 400 degrees for 25 to 30 minutes. *Yield: 6 servings.*

The **Children's Cabinet**

Frog in a Milk-Pail

A frog was hopping around a farmyard, when it decided to investigate the barn. Being somewhat careless, and maybe a little too curious, he ended up falling into a pail half-filled with fresh milk.

As he swam about attempting to reach the top of the pail, he found that the sides of the pail were too high and steep to reach. He tried to stretch his back legs to push off from the bottom of the pail but found it too deep.

But this frog was determined not to give up, and he continued to struggle.

He kicked and squirmed and kicked and squirmed, until at last, all his churning about in the milk had turned the milk into a big hunk of butter.

The butter was now solid enough for him to climb onto and get out of the pail!

"Never Give Up!"

—Frog Fables at www.allaboutfrogs.org

Entrées and Main Dishes

Sandoval's Italian Beef Kabobs

$1/4$ cup balsamic vinegar
$1/4$ cup water
2 tablespoons olive oil
2 garlic cloves, minced
1 tablespoon dried oregano
$1^1/2$ teaspoons dried marjoram
1 teaspoon sugar
12 ounces beef sirloin or round steak,
    cut into 1-inch cubes

Whisk the vinegar, water, olive oil, garlic, oregano, marjoram and sugar in a bowl. Add the beef and stir to coat. Cover and marinate in the refrigerator for at least 1 hour or up to 12 hours. (If using bamboo skewers, soak the skewers in water for 30 minutes before using.) Thread the beef on skewers, leaving $1/2$ inch between each cube. Brush the kabobs with marinade. Place on a rack in a broiler pan. Broil 3 inches from the heat source for 6 to 8 minutes for medium-rare, turning and brushing with the marinade after 3 minutes. Discard any remaining marinade. *Yield: 2 servings.*

Variation: Bottled Italian salad dressing can be used in place of the marinade ingredients.

Sandoval's Sauce

1 cup red wine
1 garlic clove, minced
3 tablespoons Worcestershire sauce
Pinch of basil
Pinch of oregano
Pinch of rosemary
Pinch of parsley
Pinch of paprika

Whisk the wine, garlic, Worcestershire sauce, basil, oregano, rosemary, parsley and paprika in a bowl. Pour over cooked steaks, roasts or hamburgers. *Yield: 1 cup.*

Chili Pie Casserole

2 pounds ground chuck
2 cups chopped onions
1 tablespoon canola oil
2 (15-ounce) cans tomato sauce
1 tablespoon chili powder
2 teaspoons brown sugar
1 teaspoon garlic powder
1 (7-ounce) can mushrooms
1 1/2 cups water
2 (15-ounce) cans kidney beans, drained
1 (10-ounce) package corn chips
2 cups shredded cheese

Brown the ground chuck and onions in the oil in a skillet, stirring until the ground beef is crumbly; drain. Stir in the tomato sauce, chili powder, brown sugar, garlic powder, mushrooms and water. Spread 1/2 of the ground chuck mixture in a baking dish lightly coated with nonstick cooking spray. Spread 1 can of kidney beans on top and sprinkle with 1/2 of the corn chips. Top with 1/2 of the cheese. Repeat the layers of ground chuck, kidney beans and corn chips. Bake at 350 degrees for 35 minutes. Sprinkle with the remaining cheese. Bake until the cheese is melted and bubbly. *Yield: 8 servings.*

The **Children's Cabinet**

Buried Treasure Cheeseburgers

1 egg, beaten
1/4 cup fine dry bread crumbs
1/4 cup ketchup
1/2 teaspoon onion salt
1/4 teaspoon pepper
1 1/2 pounds ground beef
6 slices Cheddar cheese
6 hamburger buns, split and toasted
Tomato slices, lettuce leaves, mustard, ketchup and pickles
    for garnish

Combine the egg, bread crumbs, ketchup, onion salt, pepper and ground beef in a bowl. Mix with hands until well combined. (Cover your hands with plastic bags if desired.) Shape into 12 balls and set on waxed paper. Flatten each ball to a 4-inch diameter patty. Tear 1 slice of cheese into 4 pieces and stack on top of a patty. Cover with another patty and pinch the edges to seal in the cheese. Repeat with the remaining patties and cheese. Place the patties on a rack in a broiler pan. Broil 3 to 4 inches from the heat source for 7 minutes. Turn the patties over with a metal spatula and broil for 5 to 8 minutes or until the ground beef is cooked through and no pink remains. Serve the burgers on buns and top with tomato, lettuce, mustard, ketchup and pickles. *Yield: 6 servings.*

The **Children's Cabinet**

Shark Bites

8 ounces lean ground beef
¹/4 cup bottled barbecue sauce
¹/4 cup shredded carrots (purchased or hand-shredded)
2 (8-count) cans refrigerated crescent rolls
4 slices American cheese, halved (optional)
Milk
Sesame seeds (optional)

Brown the ground beef in a skillet over medium-high heat, stirring until crumbly. Drain through a colander in the sink. Return the beef to the skillet. Stir in the barbecue sauce and carrots and remove from the heat.

Preheat the oven to 375 degrees. Unroll the crescent dough on a work surface. Separate the dough from each can into 4 rectangles. Press the perforations in each rectangle to seal. Place a rounded spoonful of the ground beef mixture on 1 half of each rectangle. Place a half slice of cheese on top of the ground beef mixture. Brush the edges of the dough with milk, using a pastry brush. Bring the empty side of the dough over the ground beef mixture. Press the edges with a fork to seal. Prick the top of the dough packets several times with a fork. Place the bites on a nonstick baking sheet. Brush with milk and sprinkle with sesame seeds. Bake at 375 degrees for 15 minutes or until golden brown. Remove the bites to serving plates. *Yield: 8 servings.*

The **Children's Cabinet**

It Is Not Goulash

8 ounces macaroni (optional)
1 pound lean ground beef
1 large onion, chopped
1 green bell pepper, chopped
2 garlic cloves, minced
2 (28-ounce) cans crushed tomatoes
Salt and pepper to taste

Cook the macaroni al dente according to package directions; drain. Brown the ground beef, onion, bell pepper and garlic in a large saucepan, stirring until the ground beef is crumbly; drain. Return to the heat and stir in the tomatoes. Rinse out the cans with a small amount of water and add the water to the saucepan. Season with salt and pepper. Cook until heated through, stirring frequently. Add the macaroni and stir to mix well. Cook until heated through and serve in bowls. *Yield: 8 servings.*

Quick and Easy Casserole

1 to 1^1/$_2$ pounds lean ground beef
Salt and pepper to taste
1 (16-ounce) package Tater Tots
1 (10^3/$_4$-ounce) can condensed cream of mushroom soup

Press the ground beef onto the bottom of an unheated electric skillet. Season with salt and pepper. Top evenly with the Tater Tots and spread the soup over the potatoes. Cook at 325 to 350 degrees for 30 minutes or until the ground beef is cooked through. *Yield: 6 servings.*

The **Children's Cabinet**

Hamburger Stew

1 pound ground beef
1 onion, chopped
1 garlic clove, minced
1 pound pinto beans, cooked, drained and rinsed
1 (4-ounce) can chopped green chiles
1 (15-ounce) can crushed tomatoes
1 teaspoon salt
$1/2$ teaspoon pepper

Brown the ground beef with the onion and garlic in a skillet, stirring until the ground beef is crumbly; drain. Stir in the pinto beans, green chiles, tomatoes, salt and pepper. Bring to a boil, stirring occasionally. Add a small amount of water or beef broth if the stew seems too dry. *Yield: 4 to 6 servings.*

Jalapeño Corn Bread

2 cups cornmeal
1 teaspoon baking soda
1 cup milk
2 eggs, beaten
2 cups chopped green onions
$1/2$ cup shredded Cheddar cheese
$1/4$ cup chopped jalapeño chiles
1 ($14^1/2$-ounce) can cream-style corn
8 slices bacon, crisp-cooked and crumbled
1 pound pork sausage, cooked and crumbled
$1/4$ cup vegetable oil, heated
$1/2$ cup shredded Cheddar cheese

Combine the cornmeal, baking soda, milk, eggs, green onions, $1/2$ cup cheese, jalapeños, corn, bacon and sausage in a bowl. Stir to mix well. Add the hot oil and stir to mix. Pour into a very hot oiled cast-iron pan. Bake at 350 degrees for 40 minutes. Sprinkle with $1/2$ cup cheese and bake for 5 to 10 minutes longer. Remove to a wire rack. *Yield: 12 servings.*

Chicken and Sausage Jambalaya

1 (2- to 3-pound) chicken
1 rib celery with leaves
1 onion, halved
1 garlic clove
2 cups uncooked white rice
1 pound smoked sausage, sliced
1 pound cooked ham, cubed
$1/4$ cup ($1/2$ stick) butter
1 cup chopped yellow onion
$3/4$ cup chopped scallions
$1/4$ cup chopped fresh parsley
2 garlic cloves, minced
1 (6-ounce) can tomato paste
1 large bay leaf
2 teaspoons salt
$1/2$ teaspoon pepper
$1/4$ teaspoon thyme
$1/4$ teaspoon Tabasco sauce

Cover the chicken with water in a large saucepan. Add the celery, halved onion and 1 garlic clove. Bring to a boil and reduce the heat. Simmer, covered, for 1 hour or until the chicken is cooked through and tender. Strain the stock and reserve. Remove the meat from the bones and set aside.

Combine 5 cups of stock and the rice in a saucepan. Cook, covered, for 25 minutes or until all the liquid is absorbed. Remove from the heat. Fry the sausage and ham in a large heavy saucepan for 3 to 5 minutes or until lightly browned. Remove the sausage and ham. Add the butter, chopped onion, scallions and parsley to the saucepan. Sauté for 3 minutes or until the vegetables are tender. Add the cooked chicken, sausage, ham, minced garlic, tomato paste, bay leaf, salt, pepper, thyme, Tabasco sauce and cooked rice. Stir to mix well. Cook over low heat for 15 minutes, stirring frequently. Remove the bay leaf and serve.
Yield: 8 to 10 servings.

Chicken Little Bits

1 cup seasoned breads crumbs
$^1/_2$ cup grated Parmesan cheese
1 teaspoon garlic salt
1 teaspoon basil
1 teaspoon thyme
1 teaspoon dill
$^1/_2$ cup (1 stick) butter, melted
6 boneless chicken breasts, cut into bite-size pieces

Mix the bread crumbs, cheese, garlic salt, basil, thyme and dill in a shallow dish. Pour the melted butter into a bowl. Dip the chicken pieces into the butter and then into the crumb mixture, coating well. Arrange on a foil-lined baking sheet. Bake at 400 degrees for 15 minutes or until the chicken is cooked through. *Yield: 6 servings.*

Note: You may freeze the chicken bits before baking and store in freezer bags. Thaw before baking.

Easy Cheesy

3 ounces cream cheese, softened
2 tablespoons finely chopped onion
1 teaspoon milk
1 (8-count) can refrigerated crescent rolls
5 slices bacon, crisp-cooked and crumbled
1 tablespoon grated Parmesan cheese

Mix the cream cheese, onion and milk in a small bowl. Unroll the crescent dough on a work surface. Separate the dough into 4 rectangles. Press the perforations in each rectangle to seal. Spread 2 tablespoons of the cream cheese mixture on each rectangle. Sprinkle with the bacon. Roll up the dough, starting with the long side and pressing to seal. Cut each roll into 8 slices. Place cut side down on an ungreased baking sheet. Sprinkle with the Parmesan cheese. Bake at 375 degrees for 12 to 15 minutes or until golden brown. *Yield: 6 to 8 servings.*

by Mary-Ann Brown

Huevos Rancheros—Kid Style

    16 ounces Cheddar cheese, shredded
    2 (4-ounce) cans chopped green chiles,
        drained and liquid reserved
    12 eggs
    Salt and pepper to taste
    6 corn tortillas
    Salsa

Spread the cheese in the bottom of a buttered 9x13-inch baking dish. Sprinkle with the chiles. Beat the eggs in a bowl. Stir in the reserved liquid from the chiles. Pour over the cheese and chiles. Season with salt and pepper. Bake at 350 degrees for 40 minutes or until the eggs are set. Cut into squares. Serve with the corn tortillas and salsa. *Yield: 6 servings.*

Crab and Parmesan Calzonelli

    1 basic pizza dough
    4 ounces flaked crab meat
    1 tablespoon heavy cream
    2 tablespoons grated Parmesan cheese
    2 tablespoons chopped fresh parsley
    1 garlic clove, minced
    Salt and pepper to taste
    Fresh parsley sprigs for garnish

Roll out the dough on a lightly floured work surface to $1/8$-inch thickness. Cut out 10 to 12 circles using a 3-inch diameter biscuit cutter. Mix the crab meat, cream, cheese, chopped parsley and garlic in a bowl. Season with salt and pepper. Spoon the filling on 1 half of each circle of dough. Dampen the edges of the dough with water. Bring the empty side of the dough over the filling. Press the edges with a fork to seal. Place well apart on 2 greased baking sheets. Bake at 400 degrees for 10 to 15 minutes or until golden brown. Garnish with parsley sprigs. *Yield: 10 to 12 servings.*

by the Sandoval Family

Seafood Cheddar Bisque

4 ounces uncooked scallops, cut up
4 ounces fresh deveined peeled shrimp, cut up
4 ounces flaked cooked crab meat
2 scallions, chopped
1 rib celery, chopped
2 tablespoons chopped fresh parsley
1 tablespoon chopped pimento
$2^1/2$ cups fish stock or clam juice
1 cup chicken broth
3 tablespoons butter
5 tablespoons flour
3 tablespoons dry vermouth
$1/4$ cup half-and-half
$3/4$ cup heavy cream
1 teaspoon dill weed
$3/4$ teaspoon thyme
$1/2$ teaspoon seafood seasoning
$1/2$ teaspoon white pepper
$1/2$ teaspoon nutmeg
Salt to taste
$1^1/2$ cups shredded Cheddar cheese
4 shrimp for garnish
Sprigs of fresh dill for garnish

Combine the scallops, 4 ounces shrimp, crab meat, scallions, celery, parsley, pimento, fish stock and chicken broth in a blender container. Process until smooth. Pour into a large saucepan. Melt the butter in a small heavy saucepan over low heat. Stir in the flour. Cook for 1 minute, stirring constantly. Stir in the vermouth. Whisk in the half-and-half gradually. Add to the seafood mixture. Stir in the cream, dill weed, thyme, seafood seasoning, pepper and nutmeg. Season with salt. Add the cheese and cook until the cheese melts, stirring constantly. Simmer for 10 minutes. Ladle into 4 bowls and garnish each with a shrimp and a sprig of fresh dill.
Yield: 4 servings.

Best Cajun Shrimp

1 bunch scallions
3 tablespoons butter, softened
1 garlic clove, minced
2 teaspoons lime juice
2 teaspoons peanut butter
1 tablespoon Cajun seasoning
3 tablespoons butter
1^1/$_2$ pounds fresh large deveined peeled shrimp, butterflied
1 large red onion, cut into pieces
1 green bell pepper, cut into pieces
1 red bell pepper, cut into pieces
2 tablespoons finely chopped fresh parsley
3 to 4 cups hot cooked white rice
3 tablespoons finely chopped fresh parsley

Cut the scallions into 2-inch-long slivers. Place in a small bowl of ice water to develop curls and set aside. Stir the softened butter, garlic, lime juice and peanut butter in a bowl. Add the Cajun seasoning and stir to mix well. Melt 3 tablespoons butter in a large heavy skillet. Heat until almost starting to brown. Add the shrimp and sauté for 2 to 3 minutes or just until the shrimp begin to turn pink. Add the peanut butter mixture, onion, green bell pepper and red bell pepper. Sauté for 2 to 3 minutes. Add the 2 tablespoons parsley and sauté for 1 minute or until the shrimp are pink but not overcooked. Remove from the heat. Combine the hot rice and 3 tablespoons parsley in a shallow heated serving dish. Toss to mix. Spoon the shrimp, onion, bell peppers and any pan juices over the rice. Drain the scallion curls and arrange on top. *Yield: 4 to 6 servings.*

by Michalle Shown

The **Children's Cabinet**

84

Stuffed Pasta Shells

1 pound lean ground beef
1 onion, chopped
1 1/2 teaspoons chili powder
3 ounces cream cheese, softened
1/4 cup taco sauce
12 jumbo pasta shells, cooked al dente and drained
1/2 cup taco sauce
1 cup shredded Colby Jack cheese
1/2 cup crushed corn chips
4 green onions, sliced
1/2 cup sour cream

Brown the ground beef and onion in a skillet over medium-high heat for 5 to 6 minutes, stirring until the ground beef is crumbly; drain. Stir in the chili powder, cream cheese and 1/4 cup taco sauce. Cook over medium-low heat for 2 to 3 minutes or until the cream cheese melts, stirring occasionally. Remove from the heat. Fill the pasta shells with the beef mixture, using about 2 tablespoons in each shell. Arrange the stuffed shells in an 8- or 9-inch square baking pan coated with nonstick cooking spray. Pour 1/2 cup taco sauce over the shells. Cover the pan with foil. Bake at 350 degrees for 20 minutes. Remove the foil and top with the Colby Jack cheese and sprinkle with the corn chips. Bake, uncovered, for 10 minutes longer or until the cheese melts. Garnish with the sliced green onions and sour cream. *Yield: 6 servings.*

by the Sandoval Family

The **Children's Cabinet**

Vegetable Pasta Italiano

8 ounces lean ground turkey
1 red bell pepper, thinly sliced
1 tablespoon paprika
1 (28-ounce) can crushed tomatoes
1 cup chicken broth
2 cups uncooked bow tie pasta
2 cups broccoli florets
1 cup cauliflower florets
1/2 bunch parsley, stemmed and chopped
1/4 cup seasoned dry bread crumbs
1/4 cup grated Parmesan cheese

Cook the ground turkey in a skillet over medium-high heat for
2 minutes, stirring until crumbly. Stir in the bell pepper and paprika.
Cook for 2 minutes. Add the tomatoes, broth and pasta. Bring to
a boil and reduce the heat. Simmer, covered, for 15 minutes.
Arrange the broccoli and cauliflower on top of the pasta mixture.
Cook, covered, for 10 minutes. Toss the parsley, bread crumbs and
cheese in a bowl. Sprinkle over the vegetables. Remove from the
heat and let stand for 3 minutes before serving. *Yield: 4 servings.*

by the Sandoval Family

Spunky Vegetable Pizza

3/4 cup pizza sauce
1 large Italian pizza shell
1 cup chopped broccoli
1 cup shredded carrots
1/2 cup sliced red bell pepper
5 to 6 ounces mozzarella cheese, shredded

Spread the pizza sauce on the pizza shell and place on a baking
sheet. Arrange the broccoli, carrots and bell pepper on the sauce.
Sprinkle with the cheese. Bake at 450 degrees for 10 minutes. Let
cool for 3 minutes before cutting into 8 wedges. *Yield: 8 servings.*

Vegetable Lasagna

1 zucchini, shredded (about 1 cup)
2 cups spaghetti sauce
8 precooked or oven-ready lasagna noodles
1 (10-ounce) package frozen chopped spinach, thawed
    and squeezed dry
1¹/₂ cups reduced-fat cottage cheese or ricotta cheese
¹/₃ cup grated Parmesan cheese
2 teaspoons oregano
1 (7-ounce) can mushroom stems and pieces, drained
2 cups shredded mozzarella cheese (8 ounces)

Mix the zucchini and spaghetti sauce in a bowl. Spread ¹/₂ cup of the sauce mixture in the bottom of an ungreased square baking pan. Arrange 2 noodles on the sauce so that they are not touching the sides of the pan. Spread ¹/₄ of the remaining sauce over the noodles. Mix the spinach, cottage cheese, Parmesan cheese and oregano in a bowl. Drop ¹/₄ of the spinach mixture by small spoonfuls over the sauce layer and carefully spread. Sprinkle with ¹/₄ of the mushrooms and ¹/₄ of the mozzarella cheese. Repeat the layers 3 more times, beginning with the noodles. Cover with plastic wrap and then with foil. Chill for up to 24 hours. Remove the plastic wrap and replace the foil. Bake at 400 degrees for 45 minutes. Remove the foil and bake for 10 minutes longer or until bubbly around the edges. Remove to a wire rack and let stand for 10 minutes before cutting into squares. *Yield: 6 servings.*

by the Sandoval Family

The **Children's Cabinet**

Terra Haute Pancakes

2 cups buttermilk or sour cream
2 egg yolks
1/2 cup (1 stick) butter, melted
1 teaspoon baking soda
2 tablespoons sugar
1 1/2 cups flour
1 1/2 teaspoons salt
2 egg whites

Mix the buttermilk, egg yolks, melted butter, baking soda, sugar, flour and salt in a bowl until blended. Beat the egg whites in a bowl until stiff peaks form. Fold into the batter; it will be thin. Cook on a griddle or in a skillet. *Yield: 6 servings.*

Note: In approximately 1930, Sue Dermody's father was in a large hotel in Terra Haute, Indiana. He ordered their pancakes and liked them so much that he paid the chef $50 for the recipe. It's been in the family ever since.

by the Dermody Family

The **Children's Cabinet**

Banana Raisin Pancakes

2 very ripe bananas
1 egg
$3/4$ cup low-fat milk
1 tablespoon vegetable oil
1 cup pancake mix
$1/2$ cup raisins
$1/8$ teaspoon cinnamon

Mash the bananas in a large bowl with a fork until smooth. Add the egg, milk and oil. Stir to mix well. Stir the pancake mix, raisins and cinnamon in a bowl. Add to the banana mixture and stir just until moistened. Heat a nonstick skillet over medium-high heat. Drop $1/4$-cup measures of batter into the skillet. Cook until bubbles form on the top and the bottoms are golden brown. Flip the pancakes and cook for 1 minute longer. Remove the cooked pancakes to a serving platter and keep warm while cooking the remaining pancakes. *Yield: 6 servings.*

The Children's
Cabinet

The Ant and the Dove

An ant went to the bank of a river to quench her thirst, and being carried away by the rush of the stream, was on the point of drowning. A dove sitting in a tree overhanging the water plucked a leaf and let it fall into the stream close to her. The ant climbed onto it and floated in safety to the bank. Shortly afterwards a bird catcher came to the tree and laid a snare made of twigs for the dove, which sat in the branches. The ant, perceiving his design, stung him on the foot. In pain, the bird catcher threw down the twigs, and the noise made the dove take wing.

*One good turn
deserves another.*

—An Aesop's Fable

Desserts and Beverages

Banana Crunch

8 bananas
2 tablespoons lemon juice
$1/4$ cup raisins
6 tablespoons quick-cooking oats
2 tablespoons all-purpose flour
2 tablespoons whole wheat flour
$1/2$ teaspoon cinnamon
1 tablespoon butter

Slice the bananas and arrange in a greased 9 x 13-inch baking pan. Drizzle with the lemon juice and sprinkle with the raisins. Mix the oats, all-purpose flour, whole wheat flour and cinnamon in a small bowl. Cut in the butter with a pastry blender or fork until crumbly. Sprinkle over the bananas. Broil until lightly browned, watching carefully to prevent overbrowning. Remove to a wire rack to cool slightly. *Yield: 11 servings.*

The **Children's Cabinet**

Noodle Kugel

3 ounces cream cheese, softened
2 (5-ounce) cans evaporated milk, chilled
1 cup cold milk
6 eggs, at room temperature
$3/4$ cup sugar
$1/2$ teaspoon vanilla extract
$1/2$ teaspoon almond extract
$2/3$ pound wide noodles, cooked al dente and drained

Beat the cream cheese in a mixing bowl until fluffy. Add the evaporated milk gradually, beating to a whipped cream consistency. Beat in the cold milk gradually. Place in the refrigerator. Beat the eggs in a mixing bowl until thick and pale yellow. Beat in the sugar, vanilla and almond extract. Add to the milk mixture and stir to mix. Fold in the noodles. Pour into a well-greased baking pan. Bake at 350 degrees for 1 hour or until the top and bottom crusts are golden brown. Remove to a wire rack to cool. *Yield: 12 servings.*

The **Children's Cabinet**

Snow Pudding

1 envelope unflavored gelatin
$1/4$ cup cold water
$1/8$ teaspoon salt
1 cup boiling water
1 cup sugar
$1/4$ cup fresh lemon juice
3 egg whites
3 egg yolks, lightly beaten
2 tablespoons sugar
Pinch of salt
$1 1/2$ cups hot milk
$1/2$ teaspoon vanilla extract

Soften the gelatin in the cold water in a bowl. Add $1/8$ teaspoon salt. Add the boiling water and stir until the gelatin dissolves. Add 1 cup sugar and lemon juice and stir until the sugar dissolves. Strain into a large bowl and let cool. Cover and chill until partially set. Beat the egg whites in a mixing bowl until stiff peaks form. Add to the thickened gelatin mixture and beat until stiff enough to hold its shape. Cover and chill until firm.

Combine the egg yolks, 2 tablespoons sugar, pinch of salt and milk in the top of a double boiler. Cook over simmering water over medium heat until thickened, stirring constantly. Remove from the heat to cool. Stir in the vanilla. Serve with the pudding. *Yield: 4 servings.*

Note: To avoid raw eggs that may carry salmonella, we suggest using equivalent amounts of meringue powder and pasteurized egg substitute.

The **Children's Cabinet**

Summer Pudding

1 1/2 pints fresh raspberries or mixed fresh berries
1/2 cup sugar
10 slices firm white bread, crusts removed
Whipped cream (optional)

Combine the raspberries and sugar in a small saucepan. Cook over medium heat for 3 minutes or until the sugar dissolves, stirring gently 3 or 4 times. Remove from the heat and let cool. Line a buttered 3-cup bowl with the bread slices, overlapping and cutting into halves to fit as needed. Reserve the remaining bread slices for the top. Remove 3 tablespoons of syrup from the cooled berries to a small bowl. Cover and chill. Pour the remaining berries and syrup into the bread-lined bowl. Top with the remaining bread slices, overlapping and cutting to fit so that no berries show through. Crimp the bread around the edge of the bowl. Top with a plate that is a slightly smaller in diameter than the bowl. Weight the plate with 2 cans or something similar to press down on the bread and berries. Chill overnight.

Remove the weight and smaller plate. Place a serving plate on top of the bowl and invert. Remove the bowl. Pour the reserved syrup on any areas of bread that are not completely soaked. Cut into wedges and serve cold with whipped cream.
Yield: 6 to 8 servings.

Note: If using blueberries, mash them slightly with the sugar before adding the raspberries.

Tiramisu

1 cup whipping cream
8 ounces cream cheese, softened
1/2 cup confectioners' sugar
2 tablespoons light rum or rum extract
12 ladyfingers, split into halves lengthwise
1/2 cup cold prepared espresso or strong coffee
2 teaspoons baking cocoa
Maraschino cherries with stems for garnish

Pour the whipping cream into a medium mixing bowl and chill until very cold. Beat at high speed until stiff peaks form. Beat the cream cheese and confectioners' sugar at medium speed in a medium mixing bowl until smooth. Beat in the rum at low speed. Fold in the whipped cream with a rubber spatula until just blended. Arrange half the ladyfingers cut side up in the bottom of a serving dish. Drizzle half the espresso over the ladyfingers. Spread with half the cream cheese mixture. Arrange the remaining ladyfingers cut side up over the layers. Drizzle with the remaining espresso and spread with the remaining cream cheese mixture. Sprinkle or sift the baking cocoa on top. Cover and chill for 4 hours or until the filling is firm. Garnish each serving with a cherry. *Yield: 9 servings.*

The **Children's Cabinet**

Oreo Cookie Cheesecake

21 Oreo cookies, crushed
1/4 cup (1/2 stick) butter, melted
32 ounces cream cheese, softened
1 1/4 cups sugar
2 tablespoons flour
4 eggs
3 egg yolks
21 Oreo cookies, broken
2 cups sour cream
1/4 cup sugar

Mix the crushed cookies and melted butter in a bowl. Press into the bottom and up the side of a 9-inch springform pan coated with nonstick cooking spray. Beat the cream cheese, 1 1/4 cups sugar, flour, eggs and egg yolks in a mixing bowl until smooth. Pour half the cream cheese mixture into the crust. Sprinkle with the broken cookies and pour the remaining cream cheese mixture on top. Bake at 225 degrees for 45 minutes. Remove from the oven and increase the oven temperature to 350 degrees. Mix the sour cream and 1/4 cup sugar in a bowl. Spread over the top of the cheesecake. Bake at 350 degrees for 7 minutes. Remove to a wire rack to cool. Chill until firm. Loosen the cheesecake from the side of the pan with a sharp knife and remove the side of the pan before serving. *Yield: 8 to 10 servings.*

The Children's Cabinet

Pumpkin Cream Pie

$3/4$ cup sugar
2 tablespoons cornstarch
1 teaspoon cinnamon
$1/2$ teaspoon nutmeg
$1/2$ teaspoon ginger
$1/4$ teaspoon ground cloves
$1/2$ teaspoon salt
2 cups evaporated milk
1 (16-ounce) can pumpkin
2 egg yolks, lightly beaten
1 baked (9-inch) pie shell
4 egg whites
$1/4$ cup sugar

Combine $3/4$ cup sugar, cornstarch, cinnamon, nutmeg, ginger, cloves and salt in a double boiler. Stir in the evaporated milk and pumpkin gradually. Cook over boiling water for 10 minutes, stirring frequently. Stir a small amount of the hot pumpkin mixture into the beaten egg yolks in a small bowl. Stir the eggs into the hot mixture. Cook for 3 to 4 minutes or until thickened, stirring constantly. Remove from the heat to cool. Pour into the baked pie shell. Beat the egg whites in a mixing bowl until soft peaks form. Add $1/4$ cup sugar gradually, beating until stiff peaks form. Spread over the filling, sealing to the edges. Bake at 450 degrees for 3 to 5 minutes or until lightly browned. Remove to a wire rack to cool. Serve at room temperature. Refrigerate any leftovers. *Yield: 8 to 10 servings.*

The **Children's Cabinet**

Kids Cobbler

$^1/_2$ cup (1 stick) butter
1 cup flour
1 cup sugar
1 teaspoon baking powder
1 cup milk
1 teaspoon vanilla extract
2 (16-ounce) cans favorite fruit, drained
Ground cinnamon (optional)

Melt the butter in a 2-quart baking dish in a 350-degree oven. Combine the flour, sugar, baking powder, milk and vanilla in a bowl and stir until just mixed; the batter will be slightly lumpy. Pour over the melted butter. Spoon the fruit on top of the batter. Sprinkle with cinnamon. Bake at 350 degrees for 1 hour. *Yield: 6 to 8 servings.*

Note: You may substitute sweetened fresh or thawed frozen fruit for the canned fruit.

The **Children's Cabinet**

Party Hat Cake

1 (2-layer) package lemon cake mix
1 tablespoon grated lemon zest
2 (16-ounce) cans lemon frosting
3 (12-inch) strawberry fruit roll ribbons

Prepare the cake mix using the package directions. Stir in the lemon zest. Divide the batter between 1 greased 9-inch round cake pan and 1 greased 8-inch round cake pan. Bake the layers using the package directions. Cool on wire racks. Trim the 8-inch layer to make a 6-inch-diameter layer. Place the 9-inch layer on a 12-inch cake plate. Spread some frosting in the middle and center the 6-inch layer on top. Cover the top and sides of the cake with a smooth layer of frosting. Score the frosting with a fork to resemble the basket weave of a straw hat, if desired. Unroll the fruit ribbons and wrap around the 6-inch layer to resemble a hat band, loosely tying at the back and letting the ends trail down the back of the brim. *Yield: 8 to 10 servings.*

The **Children's Cabinet**

Sour Cream Coffee Cake

1 cup (2 sticks) butter, softened
2 cups sugar
2 eggs
1 cup sour cream
$^1/_4$ teaspoon vanilla extract
2 cups flour
1 teaspoon baking powder
$^1/_4$ teaspoon salt
$^1/_2$ cup nuts, chopped
1 teaspoon cinnamon
$^1/_2$ cup packed brown sugar
Confectioners' sugar for dusting

Cream the butter in a large mixing bowl until light and fluffy. Add the sugar gradually, beating constantly. Add the eggs 1 at a time, beating well after each addition. Fold in the sour cream and vanilla. Mix the flour, baking powder and salt in a bowl. Stir into the creamed mixture. Pour half the batter into a greased and floured bundt pan. Mix the nuts, cinnamon and brown sugar in a bowl. Sprinkle half the nut mixture over the batter in the pan. Top with the remaining batter and sprinkle with the remaining nut mixture. Bake at 350 degrees for 50 minutes. Cool in the pan for 15 minutes. Invert onto a serving platter and dust with confectioners' sugar. Let stand for 1 day before serving. *Yield: 8 to 10 servings.*

The Children's Cabinet

Favorite Chocolate Cake

1/2 cup vegetable oil
1 1/2 cups packed brown sugar
1/2 cup sugar
2 extra-large eggs
1/4 cup (heaping) baking cocoa
1/2 cup cold water
2 cups flour
1 cup boiling water
1 teaspoon baking soda
1 teaspoon vanilla extract
Dash of salt
1 1/3 cups sugar
6 tablespoons milk
6 tablespoons butter
1/2 cup (3 ounces) chocolate chips
1 teaspoon vanilla extract

Beat the oil, brown sugar, 1/2 cup sugar, eggs, baking cocoa and cold water in a large mixing bowl until smooth. Beat in the flour until smooth. Combine the boiling water and baking soda in a small bowl. Stir into the batter. Add 1 teaspoon vanilla and salt and mix until smooth. Pour into a nonstick 9x13-inch cake pan. Bake at 350 degrees for 30 minutes or until a wooden pick inserted in the center comes out clean. Remove to a wire rack to cool.

Combine 1 1/3 cups sugar, milk and butter in a saucepan. Bring to a full boil. Boil for 1 1/2 minutes, stirring frequently. Remove from the heat. Add the chocolate chips and 1 teaspoon vanilla and beat until smooth and a spreading consistency. Spread on top of the cooled cake. *Yield: 15 servings.*

The **Children's Cabinet**

Cow Cake

1 baked 9-inch cake layer
2 to 3 cups vanilla frosting
1 baked dome cake
3 baked cupcakes
1 cup chocolate frosting
2 malted milk balls
2 black gumdrops
$1/2$ red fruit slice candy
1 pink fruit slice candy, cut into 4 pieces
Black shoestring licorice

Place the 9-inch cake layer on a large cake plate. Spread some vanilla frosting over the layer. Arrange the dome cake flat side down in the center. Cut 1 cupcake into halves vertically. Place the halves at the 10 o'clock and 2 o'clock position around the dome cake for ears. Arrange the remaining 2 cupcakes around the 9-inch cake layer at the 5 o'clock and 7 o'clock position for legs. Frost the cakes and cupcakes with the remaining vanilla frosting. Add random spots with chocolate frosting. Place the malted milk balls on the dome cake for eyes, the gumdrops for nostrils and the $1/2$ red candy slice for the mouth. Arrange the pink candy slice pieces on the ears. Cut the licorice into the desired lengths and use for eyelashes and hooves. *Yield: 10 servings.*

Note: For the dome cake, bake cake batter in a 1-quart ovenproof glass bowl.

The **Children's Cabinet**

Fourth of July Cake

2 (16-ounce) packages pound cake mix
$1^1/_2$ cups milk
4 eggs
3 cups whipping cream
$^1/_3$ cup confectioners' sugar
$1^1/_2$ teaspoons vanilla extract
$1^1/_2$ pints blueberries
$2^1/_2$ pints raspberries

Beat the cake mixes, milk and eggs in a large mixing bowl until well mixed. Pour into a greased and floured 9x13-inch cake pan. Bake at 350 degrees for 45 to 50 minutes or until a wooden pick inserted in the center comes out clean. Cool in the pan on a wire rack for 15 minutes. Loosen the edges and invert onto a wire rack to cool completely. Place the cooled cake on a large platter. Combine the whipping cream, confectioners' sugar and vanilla in a mixing bowl and beat until stiff peaks form. Remove 1 cup of the mixture and reserve. Spread the remaining whipped cream over the top and sides of the cake. Arrange the blueberries and raspberries on top of the cake to resemble an American flag, with the blueberries being the stars' background and the raspberries being the red stripes and leaving a strip of white between the rows of raspberries. Spoon the reserved whipped cream into a pastry bag fitted with a medium star tip. Pipe 6 lines between the rows of raspberries to represent the white stripes on the flag. Pipe a decorative border around the bottom edges of the cake. Chill until ready to serve. *Yield: 30 servings.*

The **Children's Cabinet**

Cookie Truffles

1 (18-ounce) package Oreo cookies
8 ounces cream cheese, softened
1 package vanilla bark

Place the cookies in a sealable plastic bag and seal tightly. Place inside another bag and seal tightly. Crush with a rolling pin into small pieces. Remove the crumbled cookies to a bowl. Add the cream cheese and stir to mix well. Shape into small balls. Melt the vanilla bark in a double boiler over simmering water. Coat the balls in the melted vanilla bark and place on baking sheets lined with waxed paper. Freeze until firm. Store in an airtight container in the freezer. *Yield: 3 dozen.*

Nut Goodie Treats

1 package almond bark
1 cup peanut butter
2 cups (12 ounces) semisweet chocolate chips
16 ounces dry roasted nuts

Melt the almond bark in a double boiler over simmering water. Add the peanut butter and chocolate chips. Cook until melted, stirring frequently. Add the nuts and stir to coat. Drop by spoonfuls onto a baking sheet lined with foil. Freeze until firm. Store in an airtight container in the freezer. *Yield: 4 dozen.*

The Children's Cabinet

My Favorite Oatmeal Cookies

3/4 cup (1 1/2 sticks) butter, softened
1 1/2 cups packed brown sugar
1 egg
1/3 cup milk
4 1/2 teaspoons vanilla extract
3 cups quick-cooking oats
1 cup flour
1/2 teaspoon baking soda
1/2 teaspoon salt
1/4 teaspoon cinnamon
1 cup chopped pecans
2/3 cup flaked coconut
2/3 cup sesame seeds

Combine the butter, brown sugar, egg, milk and vanilla in a large mixing bowl. Beat at medium speed until well blended. Mix the oats, flour, baking soda, salt and cinnamon in a bowl. Add to the butter mixture gradually, beating at low speed until well mixed. Stir in the pecans, coconut and sesame seeds. Drop by rounded tablespoonfuls 2 inches apart onto nonstick cookie sheets. Bake at 375 degrees for 10 to 12 minutes or until golden brown. Remove the cookies to foil to cool completely. *Yield: 2 1/2 dozen.*

The **Children's Cabinet**

Lace Cookies

$1/2$ cup (1 stick) butter, melted
3 tablespoons flour
1 cup sugar
1 cup rolled oats
$1/4$ cup flaked coconut
1 egg
1 teaspoon salt
$1/4$ teaspoon baking powder
1 teaspoon vanilla extract

Combine the melted butter, flour, sugar, oats, coconut, egg, salt, baking powder and vanilla in a bowl and stir to mix well; the batter will be runny. Drop by teaspoonfuls onto a cookie sheet lined with foil. Bake at 375 degrees for 8 to 10 minutes or until brown. Remove to a wire rack to cool. Peel the cooled cookies off the foil. *Yield: 4 dozen.*

by Mary-Ann Brown

Homemade Energy Bars

1 egg
$1/2$ cup packed brown sugar
1 teaspoon vanilla extract
1 cup granola
$1/2$ cup raisins or any chopped dried fruit
$1/2$ cup chopped hazelnuts
1 (6.9-ounce) package "M&M's" Plain Chocolate Candies

Combine the egg, brown sugar and vanilla in a medium bowl and stir to mix well. Add the granola, raisins, nuts and candy and stir until combined. Spoon into a generously buttered 8-inch square nonstick baking pan and pat evenly over the bottom. Bake at 350 degrees for 25 minutes. Remove to a wire rack to cool. Cut into bars. *Yield: 8 to 12 servings.*

Great Big Blueberry Muffins

2 cups flour
1/2 cup sugar
1 tablespoon baking powder
1/2 teaspoon salt
1 cup milk
1 egg
3/4 teaspoon vanilla extract
1/2 cup (1 stick) butter, melted and cooled
1 cup blueberries, rinsed and patted dry
2 teaspoons sugar

Mix the flour, 1/2 cup sugar, baking powder and salt in a medium bowl. Combine the milk, egg and vanilla in a small bowl and beat with a fork to mix. Pour into the flour mixture. Add the melted butter and blueberries and stir gently with a rubber spatula until just blended. Spoon the batter into 12 paper-lined muffin cups. Sprinkle 2 teaspoons sugar evenly over the tops. Bake at 375 degrees for 18 to 20 minutes or until golden brown and a wooden pick inserted in the center comes out clean. Cool in the pan on a wire rack for 15 minutes. Invert the pan gently over the rack to remove the muffins. Let stand until cool. *Yield: 1 dozen.*

The **Children's Cabinet**

Flower Petal Punch

14 small edible flowers
1 (12-ounce) can frozen lemonade concentrate, thawed
2 cups cran-raspberry juice, chilled
4 cups ginger ale or soda water, chilled

Place 1 flower in each compartment of an ice cube tray. Fill with water and freeze until firm. Combine the lemonade concentrate and cran-raspberry juice in a 2-quart pitcher and stir to mix. Pour in the ginger ale slowly. Place 2 flower ice cubes in each of 7 glasses. Pour the lemonade mixture over the ice and serve. *Yield: 7 servings.*

Note: You may use slices of strawberries or whole raspberries instead of flowers in the ice cubes.

Cranberry Orange Warm-Up

4 cups cran-apple juice
1 cup orange juice
1 cinnamon stick

Combine the cran-apple juice, orange juice and cinnamon stick in a saucepan. Simmer for 5 minutes. Cool slightly and remove the cinnamon stick. Pour into mugs and serve warm. *Yield: 10 (^{1}/$_2$-cup) servings.*

The Children's Cabinet

Cantaloupe Cooler

1 cup cantaloupe chunks
$^1/_4$ cup frozen apple juice concentrate, thawed
1 cup whole or skim milk

Combine the cantaloupe, apple juice concentrate and milk in a blender container. Process until smooth. *Yield: 4 ($^1/_2$-cup) servings.*

Fruity Milk Shake

2 cups whole or skim milk
1 cup chopped fresh fruit such as peaches,
    melon, papaya, pears or berries
Ground cinnamon

Combine the milk and fruit in a blender container. Process until smooth. Pour into 4 glasses and top with a shake of cinnamon. *Yield: 4 ($^1/_2$-cup) servings.*

The **Children's Cabinet**

Orange Strawberry Frosty

    1 cup orange juice
    2 strawberries
    2 ice cubes, crushed

Combine the orange juice, strawberries and ice in a blender container. Process until smooth. *Yield: 2 ($1/2$-cup) servings.*

Fruity Yogurt Shake

    2 cups whole or skim milk
    1 cup frozen fruit
    1 cup favorite fruit yogurt
    Sugar to taste
    Ground cinnamon

Combine the milk, fruit, yogurt and sugar in a blender container. Process until smooth. Pour into 4 glasses and top with a shake of cinnamon. *Yield: 4 ($1/2$-cup) servings.*

The **Children's Cabinet**

Thanks

We wish to express our thanks to
Mrs. Campbell's Kindergarten Class of 2002-2003
from Roy Gomm Elementary School
for their creative input in the following section.
The students in Mrs. Campbell's class
produced their own Thanksgiving-themed
recipe book last fall, and their thoughts
were worth sharing.

Additionally, our friend Amina Wilson contributed
to this section. Thank you all for your inspiring creativity.

Garrett Cummins	Anna O'Donahue
Cammi Garcia	Andrew Olsen
Gina Glogovac	Danyelle Peterson
Taylor Hand	Austin Salmon
Zack Haskin	Maddy Sandoval
Elijah Henderson	Eric Urban
Catherine Heydon	Sophia Vallas
Allison Larranzetti	Cody White
Emily Mannikko	Madelein Williams
Ashley McHardy	Andrew Wilson

From the Mouths
of Babes . . .

Some very original recipes

Apple Pie
by Eric

Ingredients

10 apples
9 spoons of cinnamon
A pie crust (however big the pie is!)

Instructions

" Cut the apples. Put the cinnamon
on the apples. Put on the pie crust.
Cook it for maybe about 1 minute.
Cut it up, then eat it. **"**

The **Children's Cabinet**

Turkey and Gravy
by Elijah

Ingredients

A turkey "this big"

Instructions

❝ Let it thaw out. Put it in the oven. Let it stay in there for 80 hours. Put gravy on it. Eat it! **❞**

115

Turkey
by Cody

Ingredients

Turkey

Instructions

"Buy a turkey. Stuff the turkey, then put in a pan, then into the oven. Bake as long as I'm in school (2^1/$_2$ hours) at 102 degrees."

The **Children's Cabinet**

Chicken
by Taylor

Ingredients

Chicken

Instructions

66 Catch the chicken, put it in the bag and put it in the oven for 27 minutes. Put some hot sauce then salt and pepper on it. 99

The **Children's Cabinet**

Turkey
by Sophia

Ingredients

10 cups of corn stuffing
8 lb. turkey

Instructions

"We put the stuffing in the turkey. I think that we put something on top of the turkey, but I don't know what.

Cook it probably for 8 minutes at probably 30 degrees (I think, but I don't know). We serve it by legs and wings and eat it. **"**

The Children's Cabinet

Chicken
by Emily

Ingredients

3 bones
A chicken "this big"

Instructions

" Put the bones on the chicken. First we put the chicken and then the bones on the counter. Cook it for 3 minutes. Then we let them eat it. **"**

Turkey
by Maddy

Ingredients

6 pieces of meat
3 cupfuls of sauce

Instructions

" My Grandma puts the meat in the oven and sprays the pan so it doesn't stick. Cook it for 10 minutes on warm. Put a little bit of sauce on it. Eat it. **"**

The **Children's Cabinet**

Turkey
by Gina

Ingredients

1 cup sugar
3 lb. turkey
A little bit of butter
A little bit of pepper
A little bit of salt

Instructions

66 Put the sugar on the turkey. Rub the butter on the turkey. Put the pepper and salt on it. Put it in the oven at 3 degrees and cook for 4 minutes. Cut it and eat it. 99

The Children's Cabinet

Pumpkin Pie
by Catherine

Ingredients

1 pumpkin
2 seeds
2 soups
A large pie crust

Instructions

" Mix the pumpkin together and stir it. Put the seeds in when the soup is done. Put it in the oven for it to bake for 13 minutes at 14 degrees. Nothing else. **"**

The **Children's Cabinet**

Turkey
by Ashley

Ingredients

A big bowl of red stuff
5-feet-long turkey
Skin

Instructions

" Dip a 'shot' in the red stuff and shoot it in the turkey.

Cook it for 5 hours. Take it out and put it on your plates and eat it. **"**

Mashed Potatoes
by Cammi

Ingredients

1 or 2 or 3 potatoes

Instructions

" Put them in the oven to bake for 24 or 26 hours. The oven should be warm! Take them out and smash them. **"**

The **Children's Cabinet**

Turkey
by Zack

Ingredients

1 giant turkey

Instructions

" First you take a little bit of the bones out. Then you put a little salt (about 1 spoon) and two spoons of oil. Put the salt and oil on the turkey. Cook it for about, I think, $5^1/2$ minutes at about 40 degrees. Then you can eat it. **"**

The Children's Cabinet

Sweet Potatoes
by Garret

Ingredients

3 or 4 apricots
1 cup orange juice
2 or 3 sweet potatoes

Instructions

" Put the apricots in the orange juice. Mix the apricots with the sweet potatoes. Cook it for about 50 minutes in the stove kind of hot. **"**

The **Children's Cabinet**

Turkey
by Cammi

Ingredients

A turkey "this big"

Instructions

" Put it in the oven at 48, cook it for 29 hours, take it out.

Put some gravy on it. Eat it!!!! "

Broccoli
by Cody

Ingredients

Get a broccoli

Instructions

" First we buy it. Then cut it, put it in a pot and cook it.

Pour black sauce on it just before putting it on the table for everyone to eat. **"**

The **Children's Cabinet**

Macaroni
by Danyelle

Ingredients

A little hot, hot water
2 cups macaroni
2 cups any kind of cheese

Instructions

" Put the macaroni in a bowl to cook for 1/2 hour. Pour the cheese in the bowl. Let it cool off, pour it in another bowl and that's all. **"**

The **Children's Cabinet**

Turkey
by Madelein

Ingredients

50 lb. turkey
3 spoonfuls of salt

Instructions

"You put the turkey in the oven and you bake it for 34 hours at 5 in the oven. Then take it out and have your Thanksgiving. **"**

The **Children's Cabinet**

Finger Noodles and Sauce
by Amina

Ingredients

Finger noodles (penne pasta)
Sauce (ketchup)

Instructions

" Put a pan on the stove. (Mommy's note: You might want to add water and salt to the pan.) Start the fire on the stove. Get the finger noodles out of the bag. Put the lid on the pan. Put the noodles in the pan. Now cook them! Put the water in the sink. Put the finger noodles back in the pan. Put the finger noodles on my plate. Get some ketchup out of the fridge. Put ketchup on my noodles. Eat them all up! "

Macaroni
by Andrew

Ingredients

A whole bag of noodles
1 cup of hot water
A whole bag of cheese

Instructions

" Put the macaroni in a bowl. Stir it up and let it cool down. Be sure to save some for your sister named Jessica! Eat the rest. **"**

The **Children's Cabinet**

Stuffing
by Ashley

Ingredients

10 bits of sugar
3 or 4 spoons of dough
1 more spoon of dough

Instructions

" Put it in the oven at 5 degrees. Cook it for 5 hours. Take it out and then we eat it. **"**

The **Children's Cabinet**

Macaroni & Cheese
by Austin

Ingredients

1 scoop of water
2 cups of cheese
It comes with one box of macaroni

Instructions

" Put the macaroni and cheese in a pan. Set it for about 2 seconds. Put the stove on high/low. Put it in a bowl. We eat it. **"**

The **Children's Cabinet**

Pizza
by Taylor

Ingredients

A lot of sauce
A lot of cheese
7 pepperonis
16 hot sauces

Instructions

" Cut the crust, put on the cheese and the pepperonis and the hot sauce. Put it in the oven for 15 minutes. It should be really hot. **"**

The **Children's Cabinet**

Rolls
by Anna

Ingredients

As indicated by small fingers:
"This much" (3 inches) flour
"This much" (4 inches) water
"This much" (3 inches) butter
"This much" (1-2 inches) salt

Instructions

" Put everything into a bowl, mix it, put it into a pan and then heat it up and bake it. Bake for as long as *PB&J Otter* is on TV at 102 degrees. **"**

The **Children's Cabinet**

Rolls
by Brady Bobbitt

Ingredients

3 butters
1 bread
2 cups of salt

Instructions

" Mix it in a bowl with butter and one piece of bread (use that thing that stirs it up). Put some salt in it. Roll it. Cook it for 10 minutes ('til it's very hot) and then you eat it. "

The Children's Cabinet

Pizza
by Allison

Ingredients

7 scoops sauce
Crust
3 cheeses

Instructions

" First smash the crust flat until it is 5 inches big. Then put the cheese on the crust. Cook it for 6 minutes on the stove. Cut it in pies. Eat it. **"**

The Children's Cabinet

Index

The **Children's**
Cabinet

Stone Soup tales
recipes for sharing

The Children's Cabinet
1090 South Rock Blvd.
Reno, Nevada 89502
(775) 856-6200

YOUR ORDER	QTY	TOTAL
Stone Soup tales at $24.95 per book		$
Nevada residents add $1.88 sales tax per book		$
Shipping and handling at $2.50 per book		$
	TOTAL	$

Name

Address

City   State   Zip

Telephone (optional)

Method of Payment: ( ) MasterCard   ( ) VISA
                     ( ) Check(s) payable to the Children's Cabinet

Account Number   Expiration Date

Signature

Photo copies of order form will be accepted.